DANGEROUS TREASURE

DANGEROUS TREASURE

GORDON SNELL

*For Mort and Gordon —
A thrilling tale
I hope you'll like!
With my very
best wishes,
Gordon*

Children's
POOLBEG

Christmas 1994

Published in 1994 by
Poolbeg Press Ltd,
Knocksedan House,
123 Baldoyle Industrial Estate,
Dublin 13, Ireland

A catalogue record for this book is available from the British Library.

ISBN 1 85371 420 8

Cover illustration by Aileen Caffrey
Cover design by Poolbeg Group Services Ltd
Set by Poolbeg Group Services Ltd in Stone 10.5/14.5
Printed by The Guernsey Press Company Ltd,
Vale, Guernsey, Channel Islands.

Contents

BY THE SAME AUTHOR

Cruncher Sparrow High Flyer

Cruncher Sparrow's Flying School

Tex and Sheelagh

The Joke Thief

1

Dreams of Adventure

"Brendan, where are you going?" his father asked.

"Nowhere special, Dad. Just out."

"And nowhere is where you'll end up, if you don't pull yourself together. Haven't you any homework to do?"

"I've done it."

"They don't work you hard enough at that school."

"I won't be long, Dad. I'll be back for tea."

"You'd better be. And don't go playing the fool with that Dessy, do you hear?" His father went back to reading his paper.

Brendan went out and walked along the road, his fair hair sticking out of the sides of his green peaked cap, with "Ireland" on it in white. He went towards the scruffy little park at the end of the road. He knew Dessy would be hanging around there and they could have a bit of a laugh. He and Dessy were good friends. The reason Brendan's father didn't like him was because of Dessy's brother, Mick. He had been in trouble with the guards a few times for stealing cars and shoplifting.

It was unfair to blame Dessy – but Brendan felt that his father *wasn't* fair, especially to Brendan himself. He seemed to pick on him, perhaps because he was the youngest boy. He was always saying that Brendan would never get work when he grew up, if he didn't work hard now. His father talked a lot about work. He was a journalist, who wrote for different newspapers and magazines. But not too many of them were giving *him* any work just now.

As Brendan got near the park, he saw Dessy kicking a football against a wall. Dessy was small and tough, with spiky red hair. He was always moving: tapping his feet, clicking his fingers, making sudden boxing punches in the air. He liked to wear old jeans with torn bits in them, and tee-shirts with the names of bands and singers on the front.

Brendan had tried tearing holes in his own jeans too, but his mother always said, "What do you do at that school, Brendan? Is there a class in crawling through barbed-wire fences?" Then she took the jeans away and sewed up the holes.

Brendan walked on, thinking how the bright sunshine made their road and the scrappy few trees in the park look quite cheery. He felt happy himself, as he looked forward to the coming summer and the holidays, and began dreaming up plans.

Dessy hadn't seen him, so Brendan went quietly behind him; then as the ball bounced back from the wall, he dashed forward and caught it. He put it at his feet and dribbled it towards Dessy, who tackled him. Brendan tripped and they both fell to the ground.

"Foul!" yelled Brendan. "Yellow card!"

"Shoot the referee!" shouted Dessy.

They scrambled to their feet. Dessy took the ball and they went and sat on the swings. The only other person there was a woman in a blue track suit, pushing her happily screeching daughter on the swing on the end of the row. She looked at the boys with a frown. Brendan wondered why everybody who saw himself and Dessy seemed to think that they were "Up To No Good", when they were doing nothing at all. It was just another example of the unfairness of adults.

"Only two days to go!" said Dessy. "Then, no school for weeks and weeks."

"We must make plans," said Brendan, who liked things to be organised.

"What'll we do?"

"We'll go on a fishing expedition," said Brendan. "We'll catch a man-eating shark." Dessy laughed and snapped his jaws together.

"Well, a mackerel, anyway," said Brendan.

"We could learn to drive," said Dessy. "Mick could teach us, over there on the building-site."

"We'd have the guards on us, asking to see our licences – and they'd probably nick us all for stealing the car."

3

"Mick's given up the robbing," said Dessy.

"And pigs have learned to fly," Brendan laughed.

"No, seriously he has. I heard him telling someone on the phone. He's got a new job."

"Well, he won't have time for teaching us driving," said Brendan, with some relief. "What about canoeing – in a kayak, like the Eskimos? We could learn to turn upside down like they do, and come upright again."

"As long as we don't have to drink the Liffey water on the way."

They talked happily about the different things they could do, with Brendan dreaming up more and more fantastic ideas, from making a hot-air balloon to learning tight-rope walking. As the plans got more daring, they started to swing to and fro, higher and higher. The track-suited woman looked at them even more disapprovingly, and finally she took her daughter and went away.

When Brendan and Dessy stopped swinging and got down, they grinned at each other.

"It's going to be a great summer!" said Brendan.

"Right!" said Dessy, and they slapped palms.

When the O'Hara family were having tea that evening, Brendan got some news which upset his plans. His mother's sister Maureen was coming up from the country to stay for two days, with her daughter Molly. Molly was the same age as Brendan, and he was going to have to entertain her.

The idea filled Brendan with gloom. He hadn't seen Molly for three years, and remembered her as an overactive girl with wild black hair, always dashing about the place and knocking things over. Still it's only for two days, he thought, then she'll be off back to her godforsaken village out in the far-flung countryside.

Then the news came, striking him like a thunderbolt.

"And I've a surprise for you, Brendan," his mother said. "You're going on holidays. When Maureen and Molly go home, they'll take you with them."

Brendan felt shocked. Now all his summer plans were in ruins. He had to go to the country, to a place in the middle of nowhere, full of cows and sheep and people with funny accents. Boring! he thought. Boring, boring, boring!

He tried to find some way to get out of it. "I can't go," he said. "I've got things to do here."

"What sort of things?" asked his mother.

"You don't do anything except loaf about with your mates and get into trouble," said his father. "It's very good of Maureen to take you out of harm's way for a bit."

There was nothing Brendan could do. He had to go. And now he would have to be with his country cousin, Molly, not just for two days, but for ages, with no friends and nothing to do. The future looked grim.

It didn't seem any more cheerful when he got home from school the next day, and found that his aunt Maureen had arrived, with Molly. His mother and aunt were sitting at the table in the kitchen with mugs of tea in front of them, and chattering together.

Molly sat at the end of the table, looking at a comic – one of *his* comics. His mother must have brought it down from his room. Nothing was private in this house.

"Oh hello, Brendan!" said his aunt. "Come here and let me look at you. Well, well!"

She gazed at him, smiling. He gave a thin smile and muttered: "Hello." He knew what she was going to say next – and she said it.

"Well, how you've grown, Brendan!"

Adults always said that. What did they expect you to do: shrink?

His aunt leaned forward as if to give him a kiss, and then saw him turn his head away, just slightly. "Yes, very grown-up!" she laughed, and shook him by the hand instead.

Brendan knew that Molly was staring at them, while pretending to go on reading the comic. He felt like a fool.

"You remember Molly, don't you, Brendan?" said his mother.

Brendan nodded. "Hi," he said.

"Hi," Molly answered. They looked at one another in silence. Molly was a big girl, with wide brown eyes. She was wearing a sweater with "I ❤ New York" on the front. Her black hair looked as wild and untidy as ever.

"Why don't you two go out and play?" said

Brendan's mother. "All right, Maureen?"

"Of course. But make sure you're back in time for tea."

"OK," said Brendan.

Out in the road, they walked along towards the park. Brendan hoped Dessy would be there. It would save him having to talk to his cousin on his own.

As they walked, Dessy whizzed past them on his bike, then braked quickly and turned back.

"Hello there," he said.

Brendan introduced Molly. The three of them went on to the park. Dessy produced the football from the carrier of his bike.

"Fancy a game?" he said. It was a bit of a challenge. He looked at Molly, who said, "Sure, why not?"

"I'll be in goal first," said Dessy, taking up his position in front of the wall, which had the outline of goalposts painted on it in white.

He threw the ball to Brendan, who dribbled it along, then passed it across to Molly. He half expected her to trip on it, but to his surprise she began to weave and dart about, keeping the ball under control at her feet. She ran towards Dessy, who came out of the goal to meet her. He put his foot out to get the ball, but Molly dodged past him, and kicked the ball smack into the goal.

"Good footwork," said Dessy.

"Thanks," Molly grinned.

They played for twenty minutes, then sat down on one of the benches to get their breath back.

"I didn't know you played football in the country," said Dessy.

"What did you think we did, milked cows all day?" said Molly. "We're not the culchies you think we are. I'd rather live in Ballygandon than Dublin, anytime."

Brendan was amazed. He couldn't imagine anyone really *liking* the country. "Why do so many country people come to the city, then?" he asked.

"And why do so many of them get out of it as fast as they can and head for home at weekends?" said Molly.

"They must be stupid," said Dessy.

"Anyone who stays in Dublin is stupid, I reckon," said Molly.

This is a great start! thought Brendan. What would the rest of his "holiday" be like?

It turned out to be much more exciting, however, than he could ever imagine.

2

Buskers

When the final bell rang at school on the last day of term the next day, Brendan and Dessy were among the first to snatch their satchels up and rush for the door. They joined the crowd streaming out of the main door and across the playground to the gate, cheering and jumping and clowning around.

Then as they walked towards home, Dessy said: "Holidays! Holidays! And tomorrow is Day One! What'll we do?"

"It's all right for *you*," said Brendan. "I've got to go to Culchie-land, remember?"

"When?"

"Tomorrow. We catch the two o'clock train, me and Molly and her mother."

"Well, there's the morning, anyway. See you at the park."

"See you."

But in the morning, Brendan's father said, "They

gave me some free tickets at the newspaper office. There's a new bus tour of the city starting. Why don't Brendan and Molly go on it? Then you can meet at the station to catch the train."

"Good idea," said Molly's mother. "It will give Molly a chance to see something of Dublin."

"And Brendan too," said his father. "He could do with knowing a bit more about his home city."

Brendan was about to protest, when his father went on: "And he can learn about Ballygandon too, as it happens. The tour goes to that gallery where they're showing the Ballygandon Hoard."

"All those treasures that were found at O'Brien's Castle?" said Molly.

"That's right. They're supposed to be magnificent."

Brendan remembered reading about the Ballygandon Hoard. Some children were playing in the ruins of the castle outside the village, when a stone slab on the ground fell in. There was a hollow underneath, and in it a box that had rotted away. The pile of rusty-looking bits and pieces that were left turned out to be hidden treasure: brooches and necklaces and cups and bowls. They were made of gold and silver, and decorated with jewels.

The land where the castle stood was owned by a local farmer, and he had got experts to clean and examine the treasures. There were still arguments going on about whether the hoard was his, or should be handed over to the nation. Meanwhile the farmer was making a bit of money by putting them on show in a gallery in Dublin.

"You see," said Molly to Brendan, "there's more in Ballygandon than you think. And the castle is haunted, too!"

"That's only a story," said her mother.

"No, it's not," said Molly. "Lots of people have seen the ghost of Princess Ethna."

"Only a couple of old farmers on their way home from the pub," said Molly's mother, laughing. Brendan's father and mother laughed too. But Brendan was thinking that if Ballygandon had a haunted castle, it might not be such a boring place after all.

"Who was Princess Ethna?" he asked.

Molly told him the story. Fergal, the son and heir of the castle family, the O'Briens, was going to marry Ethna, the daughter of a rich chieftain of another clan. The chieftain brought a chest full of treasures as a gift. Among them was a big carved silver brooch with delicate patterns on it in gold, and a long pin. Ethna wore it at the feast which Fergal's father held in his castle, the night before the wedding.

There was eating and drinking and music and dancing, far into the night. Fergal looked around for Ethna, but she had gone. A search was started, and she was found on a stone stairway leading up to one of the towers. She was dead, stabbed through the heart with the pin of the silver brooch.

The chieftain accused Fergal's father of arranging the murder and wanting to keep the treasure.

Swords were drawn and there was much blood spilt, and afterwards there was a feud between the families which lasted for hundreds of years.

No one knew what happened to the brooch and the rest of the treasure, but people said that Ethna's ghost was sometimes seen, wandering in the ruins of the castle, sighing and weeping.

"Don't take any notice of her, Brendan," said Molly's mother. "There's no such thing as ghosts."

Brendan smiled. Adults were always scoffing at anything strange or unexplainable. But he was determined that when they got to Ballygandon, one of the first things he'd do would be to arrange a ghost-hunting expedition.

The very next morning, Brendan's father dropped them at the offices of the bus tour company in O'Connell Street. There was a big waiting-room with benches and tables scattered with leaflets about the tours and the sights of Dublin. The place was full of people: groups of tourists with mackintoshes and cameras being herded together by bossy guides; backpackers with big boots; families with screeching children dashing around and annoying everyone.

There was still half an hour before the bus left.

"Let's go outside," said Brendan. He picked up his World Cup bag, a hold-all his mother had given him for his recent birthday. It was decorated with the Irish colours, and had lots of zips and pockets. Brendan brought it everywhere with him.

They went out on the footpath, watching the people marching purposefully along, or strolling and looking in the shop windows. Molly put her hand inside her blue anorak and took out a tin whistle. She put it to her lips and began to play. The tune was fast and happy, and passers-by turned and smiled. A well-dressed woman tourist took a coin out of her handbag and held it out, looking for somewhere to put it. Brendan snatched his baseball cap from his head and held it out, and the woman dropped the coin into it.

Molly grinned and went on playing. Brendan put his cap down on the ground in front of her. When the people saw it, a lot of them paused and threw coins in. Brendan smiled a thank-you at them.

He decided that he might have the talent for a career as a musician's manager. He could hire other players to back Molly, and they would go on tour, not just busking in the street, but playing at halls and big venues up and down the country. He was sure he could combine the job with playing football for Ireland, which was his big ambition just now.

Brendan's thoughts were interrupted by Molly, who had stopped playing and picked up the cap, which she was rattling in front of him.

"Not bad, eh?" she said. "There's enough here for some ice-creams to take on the bus with us."

There was a brightly-lit ice-cream bar just along the street. They went in and got a banana-and-raisin ice-cream, and a chocolate-and-vanilla, counting out the coins. They still had some money left over, so they bought two bars of chocolate to eat on the trip.

A tour guide with sleek fair hair gathered in a

13

pony-tail, and a superior expression, was shooing a group of tourists from the door of the office across the footpath to the bus.

"Everyone on to the bus, please!" she barked. "Take your seats. The tour is about to begin."

Brendan and Molly edged themselves to the front of the group. The guide looked down at them scornfully, as though she was going to tell them to go away. But Brendan held out the tickets. She checked them, and waved them on. Clutching his bag, he climbed on to the bus, followed by Molly. They moved quickly down the aisle to the seats at the back, and settled themselves in, still licking at their ice-creams.

A pair of tourists, husband and wife, came up the aisle, stopping every now and then to discuss which seats they would sit in. They blocked the path of the other passengers behind them.

"Move along, please!" cried the tour guide commandingly.

The pair did not hurry, but went on arguing about the merits of this seat or that. Finally the woman said, "Look, that'll do! There, at the back."

They came and sat down in the seats beside Molly and Brendan. The woman had long, straggly hair, and a dark red woollen coat. She carried a large leather handbag with a guide-book poking out of it. The man was smaller, and was dressed neatly, with a green, spotted bow tie. He wore glasses, and had a camera case hanging round his neck.

The woman was nearest to them. She took the

guide-book out of her handbag and began reading aloud to her husband. She sounded like an American.

"Dublin's tree-lined O'Connell Street is one of the widest streets in Europe, and has been compared to the elegant boulevards of Paris. It is named after the famous politician, Daniel O'Connell . . . " She stopped and glared at her husband. He was not listening, but seemed to be gazing around the bus in a fidgety kind of way.

The woman said in a rasping voice: "Harry! Am I reading to myself?!"

The man said guiltily, "I'm listening, Diane. You were talking about Daniel O'Donnell . . . "

"O'Connell!" snapped the woman.

Brendan and Molly grinned at each other. Brendan found it hard to understand why people came on a tour like this when they didn't have to – and why they then spent so much time quarrelling with each other. It was a mystery.

"Your attention, please!" The sharp voice of the guide came at them through the sound system of the bus. "Our tour is about to begin."

"Quiet, Harry!" hissed Diane to her husband, even though he'd said nothing.

The bus moved out into the traffic. The tour had begun.

3

The Treasure Hoard

As they moved through the city, the guide pointed out the buildings and monuments they passed: the statue of Parnell, the Four Courts, the Guinness Brewery. Then they crossed the river and made a stop at St Patrick's Cathedral, where the passengers got off. The guide led them into the vast, echoing church, where their footsteps made a clatter on the tiled floor. Diane peered around, checking things in her own guide-book and reading them out to Harry. He fidgeted and shuffled along, sometimes taking off his glasses and wiping them.

"You're meant to be listening!" Diane hissed at him.

"Sure, sure, sorry," said Harry.

The guide pointed out the tomb of Jonathan Swift who was Dean of St Patrick's.

"The author of *Gulliver's Travels*," Diane said loudly to Harry.

The guide was annoyed. She glared at Diane and said, "As I was about to say, Dean Swift is also famous as the author of that celebrated work, *Gulliver's Travels*. Now, everyone back on the bus, please, and we shall move on to our next stop to see the treasures of the Ballygandon Hoard."

Outside the Cathedral, Diane said "Take a picture, Harry."

"What of?" asked Harry, taking his camera out of its case.

"The Cathedral of course," said Diane. "But we need some people in it." She turned to Brendan and Molly. "You two kids, why don't you come and stand in front of the entrance there?"

Brendan shrugged and said "OK."

He and Molly made a silly face as Harry held up the camera and clicked.

"Great," said Diane. "The past and the future. Two modern Dublin children in front of the city's ancient cathedral."

"I'm not from Dublin, I'm from Ballygandon," said Molly. "Where the Ballygandon Hoard came from."

"Is that a fact?" said Diane.

They climbed back on to the bus, which went through the Liberties and then around Stephen's Green. It stopped again in one of the streets off the Green, where there was an art gallery. Hanging on the wall outside it was a banner saying, "The Ballygandon Hoard".

Once again the passengers trooped off the bus.

Inside the building they entered a large, high room with a wooden floor and white walls on which hung some big paintings with carved golden frames. They showed mainly country scenes with large houses, or family groups in old-fashioned clothes.

Inside the door stood a woman with long, smooth hair to her shoulders, carefully made up and wearing a smart tan-coloured suit.

The tour guide cried "Hello, Fiona!"

"Hello, Daphne," said the woman. Then she dropped her voice and asked "Well, how are the punters today?"

"A plodding bunch," said Daphne. "But at least no one's been sick over the steps, like last week."

Fiona laughed and said "Well, if they're all here, why don't you take them downstairs."

The treasures were on show in display cases, some on the walls and some flat on a row of tables down the centre of the room. There were spotlights on the ceiling which lit them up so that they gleamed and shone. Brendan and Molly looked around, dazzled.

As they moved round the room, they came to the case where Ethna's brooch was displayed. The carving on it looked as if it must have taken months to do.

Brendan peered closely, his face against the glass of the display case.

"I wonder if there's any bloodstains left on the pin," he said.

"You see too many horror films," said Molly. But she peered at it with interest.

Daphne the guide clapped her hands for silence.

"Quiet please!" she said. "Now I'm going to tell you something about the Ballygandon Hoard which we have been privileged to see today. These fabulous treasures lay undiscovered for centuries, buried in the ruined castle near Ballygandon, a village in the back of beyond, some eighty miles west of Dublin."

Molly snorted. "In the back of beyond, is it?" she muttered. Daphne glanced at her icily, and then went on to describe the various treasures.

When she came to the brooch, she said, "This ornament has a particularly interesting and tragic history. According to the legend, it belonged to a girl who was murdered on the night before her wedding – the Princess Emer . . . "

"Ethna!" said Molly.

"I beg your pardon?" Daphne said.

"Her name was Ethna, not Emer."

"That's right!" said Brendan, backing her up.

The tour guide said sharply, "I'll thank you not to interrupt with remarks on something you know nothing about."

"But she does know about it," said Brendan.

"I come from Ballygandon," said Molly triumphantly.

There was a chatter of interest from the tour group.

"Quiet please!" said Daphne.

"Her name was Ethna," said Molly, "and what's more, her ghost has been seen in the castle grounds, weeping and wailing . . . "

"And crying out for revenge!" said Brendan, getting enthusiastic.

Now the crowd was smiling, as well as talking among themselves about these extra pieces of information. Daphne decided that her group was getting out of hand.

She clapped her hands and cried, "It's time we moved on. I am sure we would all like to thank the gallery for letting us see the celebrated Ballygandon Hoard."

There was half-hearted, scattered applause.

The tour went on for another hour or so. Then the guide said their final stop would be at a crafts centre where they might like to buy some of the fine works on show.

As they approached the centre, Brendan and Molly could see a scuffle going on in the street outside it. There were a number of guards and police cars around. Two of the guards were struggling with a burly man in a leather jacket.

"What's going on?" said Harry. He seemed nervous. The bus stopped. One of the guards leaned in at the door and talked to the driver and the guide.

"They're getting on," said Harry.

"Sit still," said Diane.

"But . . . " Harry was rising from his seat.

"I said sit still!"

Harry sat. Molly and Brendan went down the corridor of the bus a little way, to try and get a closer look at what was happening in the street.

Suddenly Brendan said: "That bloke the guards are wrestling with – it's Mick, Dessy's brother. And there's Dessy, too!"

He dashed down the bus, followed by Molly.

"Wait a moment," said Daphne as they pushed past and tumbled down the steps. Outside, they met Dessy, jumping about from foot to foot, trying to think how he could help his brother.

"It's Mick," said Dessy. "That job he was talking about. It wasn't a proper job, it was some kind of a robbery . . . "

The guards had got Mick to the open door of one of the squad cars. Suddenly he wriggled, tripped one of them up, and slipped out of their grip. He took off down the street, running like a sprinter. There was a lot of shouting of orders, and the cars revved up and began moving off with flashing lights and hooting sirens. Two of the guards started out on foot, running after Mick.

"I must get home," said Dessy. "He might need my help."

"He won't go home, that's the first place they'll look," said Brendan.

"Well, he may need to contact me there, anyway. See you around." Dessy hurried away down the street.

"It's half past one," said Molly. "We must get to the station to meet Mam."

"We can get a bus from down the road," said Brendan. Then he remembered – he'd left his bag on the tour bus. "Hang on," he said to Molly, and jumped up the steps and back along the corridor, past the passengers who were all standing and craning their necks, trying to see what was happening outside.

He reached the back of the bus, snatched up the bag, and hurried down the corridor again. He heard Diane say "Hey kid! Wait!" behind him. Then he was down the steps and in the street again.

A guard leaned into the bus and told the driver to move off, as they needed to clear the area. The door shut and the bus moved away.

As Molly and Brendan walked quickly along the footpath, the bus passed them. They saw the faces of Harry and Diane looking out of the back window. They seemed agitated. Diane was waving her arms in the air. Brendan smiled and waved back.

"What an odd pair," he said.

"Well, that's the last we'll see of *them*," said Molly.

But she was wrong.

4

The Stolen Brooch

Brendan stared glumly out of the train as they left the houses of Dublin behind, and began to travel through the fields. A cow looked over a hedge, munching as it gazed at the train with big brown eyes. It looks dead bored, thought Brendan. And no wonder, living in the country. He stared at the cow and made a chewing face back at it.

"Watch out!" said Molly. "If the wind changes, your face will stay like that!"

"That's what must have happened to the cow," said Brendan.

The train slowed down. "We're coming to Kildare," said Molly's mother. When the train stopped, a large woman in a green coat got into their compartment. She had a bulky shopping bag which she put up on the luggage rack. Then she sat down with a sigh.

"Desperate times we live in," she announced.

"Desperate altogether."

"True, true," said Molly's mother agreeably.

"Nothing's safe these days," said the woman. "Aren't they robbing our national treasures now?"

"What's that?" asked Mrs Donovan.

"Our national treasures!" said the woman. "I heard it on the radio just now. They stole some kind of a brooch or something from the show that's on in Dublin."

"Which one?" asked Brendan and Molly together.

"That hoard from Ballygo-somewhere."

"Ballygandon!"

"That's it."

"We were there at the show, we saw the brooch!" cried Brendan.

"It was in the case, right in front of us," said Molly.

"Well, it's not there now."

Brendan nudged Molly, and said to his aunt, "Can we go and get something from the buffet car?"

"Of course," said Mrs Donovan. She took a note out of her purse. "Here, take this. And you can bring me a cup of tea, too." She turned to the woman in the green coat. "Would you like one?"

"Thanks, I would."

Just along the corridor, they stopped and Brendan said, "That's the brooch we saw!"

"Yes – Princess Ethna's. It must have been stolen soon after we were there."

"I was wondering. You know when we saw Dessy and his brother Mick, and all those guards?"

"Yes."

"Do you think that's why they were after him? Maybe that was the robbery job Mick was on."

"Could be. I wonder if he got away . . . "

"We'll soon know if he didn't. It will be on the news. I wish we were back in Dublin to find out."

"We do get news in the country, you know. They fly it in with carrier-pigeons!"

"It wouldn't surprise me," said Brendan. Then he said excitedly, "Hey! Maybe they'll want to talk to us!"

"Who?"

"The guards. We must have been some of the last people to see the treasure."

"But we didn't see anyone steal it."

"True." Brendan was disappointed. He rather fancied the idea of being called in by the guards as a witness. Afterwards he would talk to the crowd of newspaper and TV reporters outside. There would be headlines:

I SAW MISSING BROOCH, SAYS
SCHOOLBOY DETECTIVE!

"Move along, can't you?" said a gruff voice. "Some of us want to get to the bar."

Brendan looked around and saw a large red-faced man whose shirt bulged out over his trousers, glaring at them.

"We were just going," said Molly. "Hurry up, Brendan."

They walked on towards the buffet car, with the large man waddling behind them, lurching from side to side as the train gathered speed. Brendan watched the endless fields and hedges, and cows and sheep, and wished he was back in Dublin, in the big city full of excitement and danger.

When they got to the town near Ballygandon, Molly's father was at the station to meet them. He was a big smiling man with thinning red hair which stuck out in wisps from his head. He had a loud, cheerful voice, and, as Brendan found, a handshake so hearty and firm that his own hand felt numb after it.

"Welcome to Ballygandon, Brendan!" he said.

Then he hugged Molly and her mother, and took their suitcases, leading them all out of the station yard. They went across to an old blue van with "Donovan Grocers" painted on the side. Molly's father used it to carry the vegetables and fruit and other goods for their shop, and so the inside was very untidy. When Molly and Brendan scrambled into the back seat, Molly had to clear a space by putting a pile of old sacks and an empty milk-crate into the rear part of the van, where her father was loading the cases in at the back door.

He shut the doors, climbed into the driver's seat and started the engine. They moved out of the station and through the town, and were soon out in the country, bumping along the winding roads.

"All right at the back there?"

"We're fine, Dad," said Molly.

"Just fine, thanks," said Brendan, feeling another thud from the broken springs of the seat, as the van went over another pothole. The van rattled on at a hectic speed. Mr Donovan waved at tractor-drivers as they passed, and once he stopped to talk to a farmer who was wearing an old blue suit and wellington boots, and urging a small group of black-and-white cows along the road. The cows stared in through the windows of the van. From the safe distance of the train they looked stupid, thought Brendan, but close up like this, they seemed very menacing. He was glad there was a window between them.

When they got home, Molly led Brendan up the stairs and showed him into a little bedroom with two bunk beds.

"You can have whichever you like," she said, "Both my little brothers are away on a school outing – thank God only my little sister Bernie is at home."

Brendan put his World Cup bag on the bottom bunk and looked out of the window. Across the fields he saw a small hill. On top of it stood a broken-down stone tower, surrounded by other ruined buildings, their walls jagged against the sky. Empty windows gaped, and ivy climbed up the stones. Rooks dived and swooped around a few trees that stood near the walls. It looked a lonely, forsaken place.

This was O'Brien's Castle, where the Ballygandon Hoard had been discovered, and where, all those years ago, Princess Ethna had been murdered. Stabbed by the same brooch which they had seen this afternoon – the brooch which even now perhaps Dessy's brother Mick was clutching, as he hid out somewhere, on the run from the guards.

Molly's mother gave them a huge tea, with spicy sausages, round slices of black pudding, big floury potatoes, and home-made soda bread, still warm from the oven.

They sat at a big wooden table in the large, stone-floored kitchen, with a cooking range at one end. Along the wall there were cupboards and an oak dresser with plates standing up on its shelves.

A black sheepdog lay on the rug in the archway that led into the living-room. She was called Tina, and she seemed to Brendan to be the laziest dog in the world. She didn't move when people went from one room to the other, so they just stepped over her. Of course, since the Donovans didn't have any sheep, there wasn't anything for Tina to do.

The family's shop was in a one-storey building joined on to the main stone house. There they sold groceries and vegetables and fruit, tools and batteries, gas in cylinders, oil, and camping gear. The shop was also a kind of social centre for the people from the small farms round about. They would stand and chat for a long time about the latest births, marriages and deaths, and comings and goings of relations. It was a fair bet that everyone knew Molly's cousin Brendan had come down from Dublin to stay with the Donovans.

After tea, Molly said, "Come on, Brendan, we'll go and see the horses."

"I didn't know you'd got horses," said Brendan.

"Oh, they're not ours," said Molly's mother. "They just stay in our field at night."

"They pull the horse-drawn caravans for the tourists," said Molly. "Mrs O'Rourke has a few of them and she hires them out."

"They're done up like the old ones the travellers had before they got motorised," said Molly's father. "But inside they've got beds and cooking stoves and all, like a modern caravan. The tourists sleep in them, but the horses stay in our field. Except for the night when one lot didn't realise they had to unhitch the horse, and it kept walking around, and they couldn't sleep at all!"

"Molly knows all the horses," said her mother.

"Rory's my favourite," Molly said. "He's been pulling a caravan longer than any of the others. I give him a special feed of chocolate biscuits."

"I'm sure he'd prefer oats," said her father.

"No, he likes biscuits better than anything in the whole world." Then Molly turned to Brendan. "I'm sure he'll let *you* feed him too."

"Great!" said Brendan, without enthusiasm.

He didn't like to say that he'd never been closer to a horse than the grandstands at the Dublin Horse Show, where they had gone once to watch the showjumping. He didn't really *want* to get any closer, either. Horses were huge, lumbering, smelly creatures. Their teeth were long and savage, and they seemed to have far more of them than they needed. So a close-up meeting with Rory didn't appeal to him at all.

In the field, several horses stood quietly grazing or just staring into space.

"There's Rory!" said Molly, and they walked over towards a dark brown horse with a streak of white on his forehead. As they got nearer, Brendan thought the beast seemed to grow bigger and bigger. He towered above them, as Molly reached up and patted his neck.

"Hi, Rory!" she said. "This is Brendan."

"Hello, Rory," Brendan muttered foolishly.

"Here, give him a biscuit," said Molly, holding out the packet.

Brendan took one and held it out in front of him, pinched between his thumb and finger.

"Not like that," said Molly. "He might bite your fingers by mistake. Hold your hand flat, with the biscuit in the palm."

Brendan did as she said. He felt as if his hand was shaking in fear, but Molly didn't seem to notice. Rory put his head down towards Brendan's hand. His nostrils were wide, and he seemed to be breathing fiercely. He opened his huge mouth with its yellow teeth and took the biscuit whole. He turned away, munching.

"You see, he likes you!" said Molly. But Brendan doubted if that was true.

Molly took another biscuit from the packet and held it out for Rory. As he gulped it into his mouth, she said, "When I grow up, do you know what I'm going to be?"

"No – what?" asked Brendan.

"A jockey!" cried Molly.

Brendan gasped as she gave a running jump and landed sprawled across the horse's back. She stretched forward and put her hands on his neck.

"Watch out!" said Brendan. He looked on in alarm as the horse began stamping and turning around in a circle.

"Quiet, Rory, quiet. Good boy, good boy . . . " Molly patted the horse's neck, and he seemed to calm down. Then Molly said, "Right now – off we go!"

She gave a tap with her foot on the horse's side, and Brendan watched in amazement as the horse with its clinging rider set off across the field.

5

Horse in Danger

At first, Rory walked slowly, but then, encouraged by Molly, he started to trot. Round and round the field he went, going faster and faster, while Molly shouted with delight.

"Yippeeee!" she called, as they went past Brendan. "Hey, Brendan, this is the life."

As they trotted off to the far side of the field, Brendan noticed a blue car pulling up just outside the gate they had come in at. The car was drawing a horse box behind it. He saw a woman at the wheel of the car, starting to get out. She must be coming into the field, he thought.

Brendan called out, "Molly! Molly! Stop!" and he began to run across the field towards her. Molly pulled Rory up to a halt. From the horse's back she watched as Brendan stumbled over the muddy grass, slipping and sliding, and once nearly falling straight into a cowpat. By the time he reached Rory he was panting for breath and splattered with mud.

"What's up?" she asked.

"There's someone coming . . . into the field!"

He pointed to the far end. Fortunately a big bush was between them and the gate. Molly leaned sideways to get a view of the gate, then jumped quickly off the horse.

"It's Mrs O'Rourke!" she hissed, "the woman who runs the caravans. I hope she didn't see me."

Then she said, "Thanks, Rory – good boy!" and gave the horse a pat and a push on his back flank. Rory began to walk idly across the field.

Mrs O'Rourke wore riding breeches and wellington boots and a smart purple anorak. Her hair was a shiny dark red colour that looked artificial. It was swooped up in curves and curls as though it had been very carefully shaped into place.

She looked across at them, then went round to the back of the horse box.

"She saw us," said Brendan.

"Don't worry," said Molly. "She lets me come into the field to see the horses. She can't have seen me riding Rory, or she'd be shouting her head off by now. She's got a terrific temper."

Molly and Brendan walked across the field towards the gate. Mrs O'Rourke was starting to undo the clasps that held the horse box door closed. When they reached the gate she looked up.

"Hello, Mrs O'Rourke," said Molly. "We were just patting Rory."

"Is this the city cousin?" asked Mrs O'Rourke.

"That's right." Molly introduced them.

"Well, since you're here, you can give me a hand," Mrs O'Rourke said. "I've got a new horse for the caravans. Open the gate, will you?"

Brendan and Molly undid the gate and heaved it open. Out of the horse box stepped a smooth grey horse, tossing its head. Mrs O'Rourke held the bridle firmly and led it through the gate into the field. When the gate was shut, she produced some lumps of sugar and fed them to the horse. Then she took off the bridle and said, "Off you go, Jackie!" The horse moved away into the field and began chewing the grass.

"You won't be seeing much more of Rory," said Mrs O'Rourke. "He's getting too old for the caravan work. Once I've trained her, I'll use Jackie instead."

They went back through the gate and closed it again behind them. Mrs O'Rourke was about to get into the car, when Molly asked, "What will happen to Rory? Will he be put out to grass?"

"We'll see," said Mrs O'Rourke mysteriously.

"He'll miss the caravans and the people," said Molly. "He's such a friendly horse."

"Yes. Well, he's had a good life."

These words alarmed Molly.

They watched the car move away, with the empty horse box rattling behind.

As they walked home, Molly said, "We've got to save him."

"Save who?"

"Rory, of course," said Molly sharply.

34

"What's going to happen to him?"

"She's going to send him to the Knacker's Yard, that's what I reckon. He'll end up as horsemeat."

"She didn't say so," said Brendan.

"No, but she said he'd had a good life – as if it was nearly over."

"But even if that's true, what can we do about it?"

"I'll tell you later. I've got a plan."

When they got home, the light was beginning to fade in the sky. Swarms of black rooks screeched and squawked as they circled the trees, preparing to bed down for the night. The country was not as quiet as Brendan had expected – but it wasn't exactly a pleasant sound!

As they went in, Molly's mother called from the kitchen, "Brendan, while you were out there was a phone call for you. Someone called Daisy, I think. I couldn't quite catch the name, and when I said you weren't in, they just said they'd ring later."

While Molly's mother and father watched television in the living-room, Molly and Brendan played draughts on the kitchen table. They talked quietly, even though the Donovans wouldn't hear anything above the noise of the TV.

"I don't know anyone called Daisy," said Brendan. "Except a cat belonging to one of the neighbours."

"Must be a clever cat if it's making phone calls," Molly laughed. But Brendan was in no mood for jokes. "Perhaps it's a code," he said. Then he realised. "Of course – that's it!"

"What's it?"

"It wasn't Daisy at all. It was Dessy!"

"You could be right."

"How did he get the number?"

"I gave it to him. In case anything happened."

"Your parents would ring in that case."

"Yes, well, in case . . . "

Brendan looked sheepish. Molly said impatiently, "In case what?"

"Well, to tell the truth, if I wanted to go home, I was going to ring him from a phone box and ask him to ring me here and say that there was an emergency and that I must come back at once."

Molly was angry. "If you wanted to go home!" she snapped. "You mean, if you found the country so boring and couldn't wait to get back to your dirty old city!"

"Not exactly," said Brendan.

"Well, why don't you go back, right now?" said Molly. "*I* didn't want you to come here, but I was prepared to put up with it, and here you are whinging and whining the moment you arrive and getting Dessy to ring you up with made-up emergencies, when you haven't been here a day!"

She stood up, sweeping the draughts in a jumble off the board on to the table.

Brendan stood up too. "Cool down!" he hissed. "He rang himself. I didn't ask him to."

"He must be a mind-reader, then."

"No, really," said Brendan. "I don't want to go. I've no idea why he rang. But I'm afraid it must be something to do with Mick, and the robbery."

Molly calmed down a bit. "You mean maybe he's been caught?"

"Could be."

At that moment they heard the phone ring.

"Oh no!" said Mr Donovan, leaning towards the screen.

"Don't worry, it's probably Brendan's friend again," said Molly's mother. She called into the kitchen, "Brendan! I expect it's for you."

"I'll show you where the phone is," said Molly. They went through the living-room, while Molly's father grumbled as they passed between him and the screen. At the far end of the room the door led into the hallway, where there was a telephone on a small table. Molly closed the living-room door behind them, and Brendan went and picked up the phone.

"Hello, Dessy! What's wrong? Is it Mick?"

"Brendan, what on earth are you talking about?" It was his mother's voice on the other end of the line.

"Oh, hello Mam," Brendan said lamely.

"Why were you expecting Dessy?" His mother was suspicious.

"I wasn't, Mam," said Brendan. "It's just that you sounded a bit like him."

"Don't be ridiculous!" said his mother. "And another thing, Brendan – why did you get off the bus tour before it finished?"

Brendan was amazed. How could his mother

possibly know that? "I . . . We . . . It was held up . . . "
he mumbled. Then his curiosity got the better of
him. "How did you know, Mam?" he asked.

"A couple called here who had been on the tour
with you. Americans, I think. They had a
photograph of the pair of you, grinning like
chimpanzees outside St Patrick's Cathedral. They
said they thought you might like it – they'd seen
your address on your bag."

"They were an odd pair, we thought."

"Well, *I* thought it was very kind of them.
Anyway, when we told them you'd gone to the
country to Molly's, they left the photograph for you
and went away. Brendan, let me have a word with
Aunt Maureen. I want to make sure she keeps you
in order, the way you're going on just now. Your
father is out working on this news story about the
stolen brooch, or I'd let him have a word in your
ear."

"The brooch!" said Brendan, excited. "What's
happened? Have they caught . . . anyone?" He had
nearly named Mick.

"Never mind the brooch!" His mother was
impatient. "Ask Maureen to come to the phone."

Back in the kitchen, they started playing draughts
again, while Brendan in whispers told Molly about
the call. It was all very puzzling – the Americans
calling, and Dessy not ringing back. He still hadn't
rung when Molly's mother came in and said:

"It's time you were in bed. Your mother says I've
got to be firm with you, Brendan." She smiled.

"I won't be any trouble," said Brendan. Molly made a face at him.

He was in bed, listening to some music on his walkman, when there was a gentle knock at the door. "Come in!" he said.

Molly opened the door, putting her finger to her lips. She closed the door quietly.

"Listen," she said. "We can't do anything about Dessy yet, but we've got to do something to save Rory."

"When?"

"First thing tomorrow. Will you help?"

"I will, of course."

"Sound man. OK, this is what we'll do."

Brendan listened carefully while Molly outlined her plan.

They didn't realise that Molly's sister Bernie was outside, with her ear to the door, hearing everything.

6

On the Run

After breakfast next morning, Molly and Brendan
went to get fishing-rods, a net, and other fishing-
gear from the shed at the back of the house.
Brendan said he knew how to fish, though in fact
his only attempts at it had been a couple of outings
with Dessy along the banks of the canal, with a
piece of bamboo as a rod, and a string line. All they
had "caught" were some rusty tin cans and an old
sock.

He hoped he wouldn't be shown up, though in
fact the fishing expedition was really a cover story to
hide their true plan: the saving of Rory.

"We're off now, Mam," Molly called, looking in
at the door of the kitchen.

"Have a good time," said her mother, "and if you
catch anything, you can have it for your tea."

Molly was just about to close the door, when
Bernie ran into the kitchen and came over to her.

40

"I want to come too!" she said.

"Well, you can't," said Molly, "you're not big enough."

"I am, I am!" Bernie screeched.

"We don't want you," Molly snapped.

"Oh, why not take her along?" said her mother. "She won't be any trouble."

"Mam, she's such a drag . . . "

Then Bernie, beside her, whispered, "If you don't take me, I'll tell about the horse."

Molly glared at her. She realised Bernie must have listened in to their plans last night.

"You evil little pig!" she hissed. Then she said loudly, "Oh, all right, I suppose you can come along if you want to."

Bernie gave an angelic smile and skipped out the door.

Molly looked at Brendan and shrugged. She closed the door and said, "I'll kill that little pest one day."

They set out along the road, carrying the two fishing-rods, and a bag each. Molly's had the fishing-tackle in it, and Brendan's World Cup bag contained sandwiches, apples, and some cans of lemonade.

"How will you catch him? Will you ride him away? What if someone sees you?" Bernie walked beside them and kept up a stream of questions, like some quiz question-master gone crazy.

Molly stopped and said loudly, "Bernie, will you ever shut up? If you don't keep quiet, you'll give us all away."

Bernie stayed silent as they approached the gate into the field.

There were just two horses in the field – Rory, and the grey horse Mrs O'Rourke had brought yesterday. Rory was not far from the gate, standing near the hedge. They looked up and down the road, but no one was around. They undid the gate and pushed it slightly open.

"You must stay here and keep a lookout, Bernie," said Molly, as they put down the rods and bags beside the hedge. Molly took a packet of chocolate biscuits out of her bag and handed it to Brendan. Then she pulled out a piece of rope with a loop at one end.

"Let's go," she said. The two of them moved slowly towards Rory, who gazed at them as they got nearer. He put his head towards Molly, and she stroked it. "It's all right, Rory," she said. "We're going to save you."

She nodded to Brendan, who put a biscuit flat on his palm and held it out. Rory gave a snuffle with his nostrils and grasped the biscuit in his huge teeth. While he munched, Molly slipped the loop end of the rope around his neck.

"Come on, Rory, there's a good fella!" she said, pulling gently at the rope and patting his head. The horse began to move forward, and Brendan stepped quickly out of the way. They walked slowly to the gate, which Bernie was holding open. Soon, they were out on the road.

Brendan collected up the bags and rods, and he

and Bernie got the gate shut again. The grey horse was still on the far side of the field, munching grass and taking no notice at all.

"So far, so good," said Molly. "Now – down to the river!"

She gave a tug at the rope, and Rory started walking. Bernie walked beside her, and Brendan came behind, keeping a wary distance between himself and the large flanks of the horse.

Bernie started to ask questions, but Molly turned sternly to her and put her fingers to her lips, saying, "Sssssh!" Bernie nodded excitedly and put her fingers to her own lips.

The little procession made its way along the road, and then into a lane lined with high straggling hedges of wild red fuchsia. After ten minutes or so, the lane came out on to the river-bank. The water flowed along lazily, rippling here and there around clumps of rocks and glinting in the sunlight. Trees grew thick above the steep bank on the far side, but on this side there was a wide footpath and a grassy bank overhanging the river, with a high hedge on the other side of the path.

Molly turned right along the path, which led on for a hundred metres before it turned round a bend with the river, and was out of sight.

"Where are we going?" Bernie asked.

"You'll see," said Molly. She stopped and took a biscuit from Brendan's packet and gave to Rory. The horse munched contentedly and allowed himself to be led along the river-bank.

When they rounded the bend, there was a short straight stretch before the river curved out of sight again. In the middle of this stretch, sticking out into the river from the bank, was a big, tumbledown wooden shed.

"That's where we'll put Rory!" said Molly.

"What is it?" asked Brendan.

"An old boathouse. It used to belong to the Big House, before the people moved away. Nobody ever uses it now. We'll hide Rory in there for a few days."

"Then what?" asked Brendan.

"We'll try and find a good home for him, or even persuade Mam and Dad to let us keep him."

"What about Mrs O'Rourke?"

"I hope she'll just think he's wandered away, and finally lose interest. After all, she doesn't want to keep him."

They had reached the boathouse now. The wooden planks it was made of were dry and warped and had patches of moss on them.

There was a rickety door which creaked when Molly pushed it open. Inside, a stretch of earth floor ended at a small broken-down quay. Tied to it was a little boat, with its bottom full of water.

Molly led Rory into the boathouse and tied the end of the rope to a hook in one of the walls.

Then she said, "Bernie, go and pick some handfuls of grass from the bank there, and put it in a pile for Rory to eat."

As Bernie scurried off, Brendan put down the fishing-gear and turned to close the door. As he did so, he heard a voice further down the river-bank, calling, "Brendan! Brendan!"

It was Dessy. Brendan gazed in astonishment as the small spiky-haired figure in the tatty jeans came running towards him.

"Dessy, what are you doing here?" said Brendan, as Dessy stopped, breathless, in front of him.

"Who's that?" called Molly.

"It's Dessy."

"Bring him inside, quick! We don't want anyone to see us."

Dessy stumbled into the boathouse, and Brendan shut the door.

"What are you hiding in here for?" Dessy asked. "I was looking everywhere for you."

"And what are *you* doing in Ballygandon?" said Molly.

"And why didn't you phone us back last night?" said Brendan.

"I couldn't – we were on the run."

"*We*? Who's *we*?" Brendan asked, but he knew what the answer would be.

"Me and Mick," said Dessy. "He was desperate. He had to get out of Dublin. This was the only place where I knew anyone in the country. So we walked and walked, till we were out of the city; then we finally got a lift in a lorry to the town and walked from there."

"Where's Mick now?" asked Molly, as Bernie looked from one to the other of them, open-mouthed and totally bewildered.

"He's in the loft of a barn, just outside the village. I said I'd come and find you, the way you might know a better hiding-place."

"Has he got the Brooch?" asked Molly.

"What brooch?" Dessy was puzzled.

"The Brooch from the Ballygandon Hoard," said Brendan, "the one that was stolen yesterday."

"Mick never stole any brooch. He wouldn't know a diamond from a fruit gum."

"But the robbery," said Brendan. "When we saw you and him in the street there, you said he'd been on a robbery job."

"That was robbing a truck. It all went wrong, and the rest of them got away in a car and left him to face the cops."

They argued about what they should do. At first, Molly said it would be better for Mick if he gave himself up. But Dessy and Brendan said he should wait a while, till they caught the rest of the gang. Then he wouldn't have to take all the blame.

"Come on, Molly," said Brendan. "After all, I helped you hide Rory."

Molly looked doubtful, but she finally agreed. But where could they hide Mick? If he stayed in the barn, the farmer would be bound to find him sooner or later.

Then Brendan had an idea. "How about hiding him here?"

"Great idea!" said Dessy.

"You said nobody ever came here," said Brendan. "And besides, Mick could look after Rory, as well."

46

Molly thought about it for a while and then said, "Well, all right. Does he know anything about horses?"

"Oh sure," said Dessy. "He goes to the races all the time."

Before Molly had time to say anything more, Dessy was at the door, saying, "I'll go and get Mick now. The barn's not far away, and we can get here across the fields." Then he was gone.

Molly and Brendan settled down to wait. Brendan took some apples out of his bag. He gave one to Molly and offered one to Bernie. She shook her head and began to snivel.

"What's the matter?" Molly was annoyed. "You insisted on coming with us, why are you bawling?"

"I want to go home," Bernie wailed. "I don't want to meet that caramel man."

"What's she on about?" Brendan asked.

"She means 'criminal'," said Molly. Then as her sister began to wail even more loudly, she said, "Calm down, Bernie, it's all right. You won't have to meet him. I'll take you out. We'll go along the river-bank and do some fishing. OK?"

Bernie nodded, and her wails became a quiet snuffle.

"I'll come too," said Brendan, who didn't fancy being left alone with Rory in case he stampeded or something.

"All right," said Molly. "We'll go down along the bank so we can still keep an eye on the boathouse – then when we see Dessy come back, I can go and see

47

them in. I don't want them to frighten Rory."

Rory looked happy enough, chewing the pile of grass, so they closed the door and moved along the bank.

Molly soon realised that Brendan hardly knew the first thing about fishing. "Well, I guess you don't get much chance at real fishing, being in the city and all," she said.

"We have a different kind of rod, on the canal," said Brendan lamely.

"Let me show you our kind," said Molly. She produced a tin from the bag and opened it. Inside there was a mass of wriggling worms.

"Could you pick me out one of those," she said, holding out the tin.

Brendan had to do it. Trying to hide his disgust, he put his hand into the tin and gingerly picked out a slimy worm.

"Thanks," said Molly casually, as she took it and speared it on the hook. Then, expertly, she took hold of the rod, drew it back and then flicked it forward again. The line arched out over the river, and the hook plopped down into the water.

"See, there's nothing to it," Molly smiled. "Now you have a go."

She gave Bernie her rod to hold, while she got Brendan's hook baited. Brendan drew his rod back, but couldn't flick it forward again. He looked behind him and saw that the hook had got caught in the hedge. As he was disentangling it, they heard a voice from along the bank, calling, "Hi there, kids! Having fun?"

They looked, and saw coming towards them the two tourists from the bus, Diane and Harry.

7

Hidden Treasure

Brendan and Molly stared as Diane and Harry came nearer. What could they be doing here? These total strangers had first called at Brendan's house in Dublin, and now here they were in Ballygandon.

They were dressed as they had been on the bus, except that Harry now wore a bright red bow tie instead of a green one. Diane's hair was as straggly as ever, and she still carried the big leather handbag.

"How nice to see you again," said Diane. She smiled and turned to Harry. "Isn't it nice, Harry?"

Harry hastily said, "Oh . . . yeah. Real nice." He smiled too, and nodded his head up and down.

"Hello," said Molly warily.

"We heard you called at our house in Dublin," said Brendan.

"That's right," said Diane, "we wanted to give you the photograph we took."

"Thanks," said Brendan.

"We wondered how you found the address," said Molly.

"It was on that nice bag of yours, the one you left behind on the bus," said Diane. She pointed at Brendan's World Cup bag, lying on the river-bank. "We were going to return it to you. Then you came back for it yourself."

There was a silence. Diane and Harry stood there, smiling. Brendan noticed that Harry's eyes kept glancing towards the bag.

"We decided to take a train-ride to the country today," said Diane, "and suddenly, Harry said, 'Say, ain't we near Ballygandon, where that nice girl we met comes from?' So we got off at the town, and caught a cab here, just to say Hello."

"Just to say Hello," Harry echoed.

"We showed your picture to the people in the pub, and they said they'd seen you setting out with your fishing-rods. Have you caught anything yet? Maybe I could have a look . . . " She bent down towards Brendan's bag.

Molly laughed. "Oh, we couldn't put fish in *there*! Brendan would go bananas! He just loves that bag."

Diane looked annoyed, though she kept smiling. "It *is* a lovely bag."

"Lovely!" said Harry, gazing hard at it.

Brendan was puzzled. Why were they so interested in his bag? He picked it up and put it under his arm.

"I'd love to get one like it, as a souvenir to take

home. Could I have a look at it?" She held out her hand.

Brendan clutched the bag tightly in both hands, holding it towards her. She stared at it, still smiling, then said, "I'd like to feel the weight of it myself, if you don't mind."

Brendan still clutched the bag, without releasing his grip. Diane reached towards it. She took hold of the bag. Brendan held on. Diane's smile was icy. She stared hard into his eyes. Harry began to shift nervously from foot to foot.

"I only want to hold it," said Diane. "I'm not going to run away with it."

As Brendan stared at her, he realised that that was exactly what Diane was going to do. He didn't let go his hold on the bag. Neither did Diane. They must have stood fixed in that position, not moving, for ten seconds – but it seemed longer. Then, suddenly, Harry stepped forward and snatched at the bag.

"Give it here!" he snapped.

"No!" shouted Brendan, as Harry grabbed hold of the bag. Brendan hung on to it.

"You fool!" said Diane to Harry, "he'll never give it to us now."

"Then we'll have to take it!" Harry snarled, giving a heavy pull at the bag. A tug-of-war began, with Harry grasping one end of the bag, and Molly joining in to help Brendan.

"Stop, stop!" yelled Diane, seeing that Molly and Brendan would never let go. The tug-of-war went on.

"Listen, we only want to look in it!" Diane said. "Something of ours got into it, by mistake. We'll give it back. I promise you!"

Brendan and Molly hadn't time to stop and wonder what she meant, because Harry kept on tugging at the bag like a fierce terrier.

"Hand it over! Hand it over!" he said.

Brendan pretended he was loosening his hold on the bag, and Harry stepped back across the path, still pulling, with Diane holding on to him. Then Brendan and Molly gave a sudden jerk on the bag, which took Harry by surprise. He lost his grip on the bag and staggered backwards. He held on to Diane, but lost his balance and fell into the hedge, taking Diane with him. They both cursed and swore as brambles scratched them and nettles stung.

"Run for it!" said Molly, and the three of them started off down the path. They ran past the boathouse and round the bend of the river where they couldn't be seen by Harry and Diane.

"Quick!" said Molly. "There's a gap in the hedge here. Get into the field and duck down."

She lifted Bernie through the gap and followed her, with Brendan just behind, still clutching his bag. They crouched down behind the hedge, breathing heavily.

"Come on! Come on!" they heard Diane shouting.

"I'm bleeding!" Harry whined.

"It's just a scratch," said Diane. "Come on, we've got to catch up with them. They ran off along the bank here."

Now Diane and Harry had rounded the bend and were standing on the path, just the other side of the hedge. Brendan peered through the tangled branches. He could have reached through and touched them.

"They've gone round the next bend. Hurry!" said Diane.

"I *am* hurrying!" said Harry. Then they went on along the bank and round the next bend.

"Now's our chance!" said Molly. "We'll run back and hide in the boathouse."

They scrambled back through the hedge and ran up the path. Molly opened the door and pushed Bernie in ahead of her. Rory was standing calmly chewing grass. He looked up, then went on chewing.

Brendan was just going to enter the boathouse, when he heard voices along the bank. He could just see Harry and Diane, with their backs to him, talking to two people, a man and a boy. It was Mick and Dessy.

He heard Diane say, "Pardon me, did you see three kids running along here? Is there anywhere they could have gone, away from the river?"

Dessy looked past Harry and Diane and saw Brendan at the door of the boathouse. Brendan put his finger to his lips, then pointed away across the fields.

Dessy said brightly, "Oh yes, we saw them all right. They went through that gate further along the path and away across the fields."

"Thanks, kid," said Diane. "Come on, Harry." The two of them hurried down the path and stopped at the gate. They started to heave it open. Brendan went into the boathouse, and soon Dessy and Mick arrived at the door. They came in, and Brendan shut the door.

"What was all that about?" Mick growled.

"Ask Brendan," Dessy shrugged.

Brendan and Molly explained what had happened on the river-bank, and how they had first met Harry and Diane.

"Why did they want your bag?" Dessy asked.

"That's what we're going to find out," said Brendan.

He put the bag on the ground. One by one he began to open the zips of all the little side pockets. There was nothing there. Then he pulled open a zip at the end of the bag, where there was another pocket. He felt inside and gave a cry of pain. He pulled out his hand. His finger was bleeding.

"What is it? Are you all right?" said Molly.

"I'm fine," said Brendan, sucking his finger. "Tip the bag up and see what's in that pocket."

Molly turned the bag over and shook it. The packet of sandwiches and the fruit fell out of the main part, and then as Molly shook some more, something fell out of the end pocket on to the ground. They all gazed at the object, which lay on the earth, gleaming and silvery.

It was the brooch from the Ballygandon Hoard.

Mick broke the silence. "What's that then?" he asked.

Brendan and Molly told him. Then Brendan said, "They must have taken it from the exhibition, and had it with them when they got on the bus."

"But why did they put it into your bag?" Dessy asked.

Molly and Brendan thought for a moment, and then Molly said, "Remember when we saw the guards trying to arrest Mick, and the bus stopped. We thought the guards were going to get on. Then we got off the bus to have a look."

"Diane and Harry must have thought the guards were getting on too," said Brendan. "They were afraid everyone would be searched, so they slipped the brooch into my bag, thinking they wouldn't look very hard into that. Then when the search was over, and the tour went on, they'd wait till we were looking at something else, and sneak the brooch back again."

"No wonder they looked so shocked when you took the bag and went off," said Molly. She bent down and picked up the brooch, holding it in the flat of her hand. It lay there, with its curved horseshoe shape and the elaborate design of lines that twisted and scrolled in and out of each other to form a complicated pattern. There were precious stones set into the pattern, and hinged to the top of the horseshoe was the long, sharp pin. The pin that had pierced Brendan's finger. The pin that had stabbed Princess Ethna's heart all those hundreds of years ago.

"It's beautiful," said Molly.

"Worth a few quid, too, I'd say!" said Mick. "Wish I knew where we could flog it."

"We thought you'd stolen it, at first," said Brendan.

"Not my style," said Mick. "Mind you, now we've got it, I could make inquiries. I've got certain friends, you know what I mean."

Brendan knew exactly what Mick meant. But letting Mick contact those friends would only get him into trouble, and involve all the rest of them, too. Suddenly in his mind, Brendan could see them all lined up in the dock, in court, with a frowning judge in his red robes and white wig banging down his wooden hammer on the bench saying, "Guilty! Guilty! Guilty!"

"We'll have to hand it in to the guards," he said.

"Anyway, it's too well known to try and sell it," said Molly, "even if we wanted to."

"Hang on," said Mick. "Don't bring the guards into this."

"He's right," said Dessy. "They know Mick's on the run, they know he's connected with us. They'll think he nicked it."

"But we'll tell them all about Harry and Diane," said Molly.

"And suppose they don't find them?" said Mick. "They're probably well away from here by now. The guards will think you made it all up, to cover for me."

Molly and Brendan looked at each other. Then

Dessy said, "Please, don't bring the guards in."

"OK," said Molly, "I've got an idea. There's no way we can hang on to it, right? They're bound to track it down in the end. So let's hide it somewhere, then ring the guards without saying who we are, and tip them off where it is."

"Good idea," said Brendan. "But where shall we hide it?"

"In the ruined castle," said Molly. "We'll go there tonight."

8

The Haunted Castle

They shared out the sandwiches, and promised to bring some food and if possible two sleeping-bags to the boathouse later on.

"What about him?" asked Mick, pointing at Rory.

"We'll bring some food for him as well," said Molly.

"He won't need a sleeping-bag." Brendan smiled.

"Stop joking me," said Mick. "I meant what are you going to do with him?"

"He's staying here," said Molly. "You can keep an eye on him. He's quite friendly."

"You can't expect us to spend the night with that great lumbering beast," said Mick. "He might stampede, and kick us to death."

"Not unless you frighten him," said Molly. "Anyway, there's nothing else we can do. He's in hiding like you."

"And he was here first," said Brendan.

He zipped the brooch back into the pocket of his bag, and they left the boathouse, with Mick still grumbling and Dessy trying to calm him down.

When they reached home Molly's father was out in the van and her mother was out in the shop. "Well, have you got something for our tea?" she asked.

Molly looked blank for a moment, then remembered. "Oh – sorry, Mam, no. The fish just wouldn't bite. Can we go and make some more sandwiches? We're starving."

"I thought I made you enough," said her mother. "But all right, if you're still hungry."

They were moving towards the door at the back that led into the house, when Molly's mother said, "Enjoy yourself, Bernie?"

"Oh yes!" said Bernie eagerly. "We went down to the river, and we met . . . " She caught sight of Molly and Brendan glaring at her. "We met a . . . a fish-man."

"A fisherman," said her mother. "I hope he was luckier than you were."

"Yes, he caught a few," said Molly quickly. "He got the best spot."

She took Bernie's hand and began to lead her into the house. Suddenly the shop door opened wide and the bell clanged. Mrs O'Rourke marched in.

"This is too much!" she said. "Horse-rustlers, Mrs Donovan, that's what we've got now. Horse-rustlers!"

"What's the matter?" asked Molly's mother.

"We'll see you later, Mam," said Molly, opening the door into the house.

"Wait!" barked Mrs O'Rourke. "Maybe you children have seen him? You were always in the field, feeding him."

"Seen who, Mrs O'Rourke?" asked Molly innocently.

"Rory, of course! My horse, Rory! He's gone. Disappeared."

"He must have broken through the fence," said Molly's mother.

"Perhaps you left the gate open," said Molly politely.

"I did no such thing!" Mrs O'Rourke snorted. "He's been stolen, I tell you."

"That's dreadful!" said Molly.

"Who would do a thing like that?" asked Brendan. They both glared at Bernie again, just in case she was going to say something. She stayed quiet.

"Well, if you see him, let me know at once," said Mrs O'Rourke. She turned and stamped out of the shop.

"I never liked that woman," said Molly's mother. "But still, I hope the horse hasn't come to any harm."

He'd come to a lot more harm if we'd left him where he was, thought Molly, as she and Bernie and Brendan went through into the house.

They started to make sandwiches with some ham they found in the fridge, and then with peanut butter and jam. These looked so tasty, they decided they would have to test them. They ate one each and started to make some more. Soon the bread ran out, and they used crispbread instead, but it broke easily, and the resulting "sandwiches" looked very messy. Still, they were something for Mick and Dessy to eat.

Molly found half a sponge cake as well, and they put all the food into a plastic bag, which they put in Brendan's bag. They put in two cans of lemonade, and Molly went out to the shed and put several scoops of oats into another bag for Rory. They rolled up two sleeping-bags belonging to Molly's brothers, and strapped them to the carrier of Molly's bike.

Brendan put his bag on one of her brother's bikes, and the two of them prepared to cycle off down the lane behind the house. But first they had to swear Bernie to secrecy.

"If you say anything, the ghost of Princes Ethna will come and haunt you," said Molly. "We've got her brooch, so she'll do anything we tell her."

Bernie gazed at her in fear, her mouth and eyes wide open. Brendan thought he saw tears beginning to well up in her eyes, so he added hastily, "Of course, she wouldn't haunt a member of our gang, Bernie. And you're in our gang now, aren't you?"

Bernie went on staring at them, then nodded uncertainly.

"Oh yes," said Molly. "You're one of us. The Ballygandon Brooch Gang."

"The most feared horse-rustlers in the west," said

Brendan. "Put it there, partner!" He held out his hand. Bernie took it and shook hands. She was grinning broadly now.

"See you later," said Molly. "You-all stay cool now, partner."

Bernie nodded again and waved as they rode away. Then she went into the shop to join her mother.

Mick didn't think much of the food supplies, and said he could have done with something stronger than lemonade. But there was nothing he could do about it.

"What time will you be at the castle?" asked Dessy.

"About ten, when it's getting dark," said Molly.

"See you there," said Dessy.

"Here!" said Mick. "You can't leave me with that great galumphing brute!"

Molly and Brendan left them arguing.

They said goodnight to Molly's mother and father, saying that they were very tired.

"It's hard work, catching fish!" said Molly's father, laughing at his own joke. "Sleep well!"

They waited in Brendan's room, looking out of the window at the ruined castle. The light began to fade. The moon became visible, already high in the sky. It was nearly full. Clouds skimmed across it, as if chasing each other through the sky. The broken walls of the castle looked black and looming, standing up on their small hill.

Brendan took the brooch out of the pocket of his

bag and held it out. "There couldn't really be a curse on it, could there? I mean, she wouldn't really come after us?"

"Princess Ethna? No, of course not," said Molly, trying to sound brave. "We're on her side, anyway. It's Harry and Diane she'd come after."

"So you believe she does haunt people?"

"I didn't say that," said Molly. "I don't believe in ghosts, not really. But people round here say they've seen and heard strange things in that castle."

In spite of himself, Brendan shivered. The brooch felt cold in his hand. He put it down on the window-sill. They both gazed at it, thinking about its unlucky owner.

Then in a business-like way, Molly said, "Nine-thirty! Time to go!"

Brendan put the brooch in the pocket of his anorak, and they began to creep slowly down the stairs. They stopped in the hallway. The door into the living-room was closed, and they could hear the television. There was a game show on, with the kind of frantic audience that bursts into screams of laughter every ten seconds or so. Between the laughs, they could hear the steady sound of Molly's father, snoring. They tiptoed past the door, and slowly, silently, opened the front door.

They turned down the lane at the side of the house and climbed into a field. They had decided to go across country to the ruined castle, so that no one would see them. The light was fading fast, and it took them longer than they expected to climb over gates and fences and tramp across the fields. Here and there, trees stood out like dark watchful sentries. A sheep startled them, coughing behind a hedge. Sometimes they seemed to hear a rustling behind them. They looked round, but could see nothing, except the odd cow standing like a statue.

It was nearly dark by the time they reached the bottom of the hill.

They climbed steadily, without speaking, stumbling on the rough ground covered with clumps of thick grass. They stopped at the top, and crept through a gap in the broken wall of the castle. They crouched behind the wall. The moon was behind them, so they were hidden in dark shadow.

Suddenly there was a sharp, hissing sound from not far away. They both gave a cry of shock.

"Ssssh!" hissed a voice. "It's me – Dessy."

"You gave me a fright!" said Brendan.

"Me too," said Molly.

Now they could see Dessy creeping towards them, along the wall. He crouched down beside them. "You're late!" he whispered. "This place is dead spooky when you're on your own, I'll tell you that for nothing."

"Never mind, we're here now," said Brendan in a firm voice. But secretly, he thought the place was spooky enough, even with three of them here.

"Let's have a look around," said Molly. "Then we can find the best place to hide the brooch."

They moved among the ruined walls and rooms, clambering over fallen stones and sometimes nearly tumbling into holes where the ground had fallen away. They came to what had been a big chamber, with a huge arched stone window, its glass long gone, still standing at one end. It looked like the window of a church. The moon came through it, throwing the shape of an arch on to the broken stone floor.

"Let's hide it there, just under the window," said Brendan.

They moved slowly across the floor of the chamber till they were below the window. As they crouched down, Brendan took the brooch out of his pocket and handed it to Molly. Then he got a penknife from his other pocket and began scraping away a shallow hole in the earth. He reached out for the brooch.

"Ouch!" said Molly. She looked at her hand. There was a spot of blood where the pin had pricked her.

"First you, then Molly," said Dessy gloomily. "Maybe the brooch does have a curse on it."

"That's right, cheer us up, won't you?" said Brendan nervously. But he was very careful when he took the brooch from Molly and laid it in the hole. He pushed back the earth on top of it, then put a small flat stone on top.

"That's it, then," he said.

"Let's go," said Molly.

They made their way out of the chamber and moved through the ruins in the moonlight. They came to the gap in the wall where they had come in.

The wind was rising, and there was a sighing sound from a tall tree outside the wall.

A sighing sound . . . and something else!

All three of them heard it at the same time. The sound of slow, heavy breathing, just on the other side of the gap.

9

Ghosts in the Air

They looked at one another wildly.

"The Ghost!" Dessy whispered, his hand to his mouth.

"Run for it!" whispered Brendan – but he found he couldn't move. All of them crouched there as though they were stuck to the ground.

Then they heard a familiar voice, very out of breath, "My heart! It's going to give out!" Then there was a groan. It was Harry.

The three of them smiled with relief. On the other side of the wall they heard Diane's voice saying sharply, "Nonsense! A little climb up a hill! Pull yourself together! We've got to find those kids."

"Are you sure they came this way?" Harry asked.

"Of course they did. We saw them in the field at the bottom of the hill. Now, let's go in. We can get through this break in the wall. You go first, so I can make sure you won't run out on me."

Molly beckoned. They began to creep along inside the wall till they came to a cave-like place going back into the stones. It had once been a huge fireplace, big enough for at least ten people to stand up in. There was a hole in the top of it where the chimney had once been, and looking up through it they could see the stars, with the clouds racing across them. They crouched down at the very back.

They could hear Harry's voice: "Diane, I'm stuck, help me out, will you?"

"You can't be, you nerd!" said Diane. "I'll give you a push."

There was a gasp from Harry, and then Diane said, "There, you're through! Now I'm coming after you. See it's easy! Now, I'll just get that torch . . . "

Suddenly, a powerful beam of light shone across the ruins. It lit up part of the broken-down wall opposite the fireplace. It travelled along the wall to the corner, then along the next wall. They shrank back into the corner of the fireplace. The light reached the far side of their hiding-place and stopped. Then it moved towards them. Luckily the torch was shining at an angle, from the far end of the room, and so they stayed in shadow.

"No sign of them here," said Diane. "Let's go through."

They could see the pair moving haltingly across the broken floor, shining the torch in front of them. They went through an arch in the far wall and into the next part of the castle.

"Come out, kids! We know you're here

someplace!" Diane called. "Just give us the brooch you stole from us, and you'll come to no harm."

"The brooch *we* stole!" whispered Molly. "She's got a nerve!"

They heard Harry say, "I guess they've gone, Diane. Let's get out of here, before. . . "

"Before what?" snapped Diane.

"Well, you know what they say about the castle. People have seen things . . . "

"Oh come on, Harry! You don't mean to tell me you believe those ghost stories?"

"No, of course not, but all the same . . . "

"Shut up, and keep looking."

Dessy said, "Time to make our getaway."

"Wait a moment," said Molly. "I've got an idea. Let's have a bit of fun." She produced the tin whistle from the pocket of her anorak.

"What are you going to do?" asked Brendan.

"Give them some spooky sounds of those ghosts they don't believe in." She put the whistle to her mouth and made a high, sighing sound with it. Then another. They listened.

"Did you hear that?" Harry asked nervously.

"Calm down, it's just the wind," said Diane.

Molly blew on the tin whistle again. This time it was a low note, which moved up the scale to become a kind of screech. She repeated the sound. Brendan and Dessy grinned.

"That's no wind . . . " they heard Harry say.

"What else can it be?" Diane sounded a bit nervous herself.

"I don't know," said Harry, "and I'm not staying to find out!"

"Come back!" cried Diane, as they heard Harry running and stumbling about.

"I can't find the door!" he shouted. "They've got us cornered! Help!"

"Stay still!" said Diane. Then there was a loud cry from Harry. After that they heard him whimpering.

"I've fallen down a hole!" he said. "Something pushed me!"

"It's only a bit of a cave-in in the floor," said Diane. "Stand up and I'll help you out."

Molly gave another low, moaning sound on her tin whistle. Harry sobbed, "There it is again! They've come to get me!"

"Shut up and give me your hand," Diane said. "Now, put your foot on the side and push up. OK – now!"

There were grunts and panting sounds, and finally Diane said, "There! You're out!"

"My ankle's broken!" wailed Harry.

"Nonsense! Stand up! There you are. You've just twisted it a little. I don't know why I put up with you. We've made enough noise to wake the dead."

"Don't say that!" Harry moaned.

"Those kids will be half way home by now. I'm sure I was right. They came up here to hide the brooch so we wouldn't find it. But I've got another little plan which will make them tell us. Just wait and see!"

They crouched back into their hiding-place again,

as Diane and Harry came back. This time Diane was shining the torch on the uneven ground, as Harry limped along beside her. They reached the gap in the wall and went through it.

Brendan, Molly and Dessy crept out of their fireplace and along the wall. They peered through the gap. They could see the pool of light from the torch moving slowly down the hill, with the two dark figures stepping carefully behind it.

"Bye! See you later!" said Brendan quietly.

"Not if we see them first!" laughed Molly.

"That was great ghosting," said Dessy, "you almost had *me* scared."

"Any time you need a haunt, just ask!" said Molly. She blew another weird moan on her tin whistle.

From somewhere in the castle, there came an answering moan. Brendan felt himself go cold. Dessy's hair stood up even more spikily than usual. Molly went pale. There was silence. They listened. But they could hear nothing except the wind in the tree nearby.

"It was an echo," said Molly.

"Yes, that's what it was – an echo!" Brendan agreed eagerly.

"Of course, an echo!" Dessy mumbled. But none of them sounded completely sure.

They looked down the hill. The torchlight and the two figures had gone. They squeezed through the gap and began to make their way home.

Next morning, Molly and Brendan managed to

save some food from breakfast and put it in a bag for Dessy and Mick in the boathouse. Molly scooped out some more oats too, for Rory.

They planned to cycle down there first, and then go on towards the next village. There was a telephone box out on the country road, and they would phone the guards from there and tell them about the brooch. They were afraid they'd be overheard if they phoned from home, and spotted if they used the village phone box. Brendan wished he had one of those neat mobile phones you saw people using. He imagined himself as a high-powered businessman in a slick suit, turning away from the lunch table and saying, "Excuse me, I've just got to call New York."

But for the moment, calling the guards was enough of a problem. He had been trying to practise talking in a deeper voice, and putting on accents. He and Molly had had a rehearsal that morning.

First Brendan tried a fancy English accent, "I say, old chap, got a piece of jolly old information for you . . . "

"They'll just think you're a twit!" said Molly.

"All right, how about this?" Brendan tried to imitate Germans he had seen in war movies, "Achtung! Vee have news vot you vill vant to know . . . "

This just gave Molly a fit of giggling.

"You try, then!" said Brendan, huffily.

"They're more likely to recognise me, I'm local," said Molly.

Brendan tried various other voices, which only

made Molly laugh more. In the end they decided that broad Dublin would be as good as any.

They were just getting the bikes ready in the yard when Molly's mother came out. "Have you seen Bernie?" she asked.

"Not since breakfast, Mam," said Molly.

"She's not in her room," said Molly's mother, "and I can't find her anywhere in the house. I've called her, and there's no answer. That child is always wandering off."

"I'm sure she's OK , Mam," said Molly, anxious to be off.

"Oh yes, she's probably up to some mischief somewhere, no doubt. Listen, I can't leave the shop just now. Would you two have a scout round in the village and see if you can find her? And when you do, send her back home right away."

"OK, Mam." As her mother went inside again, Molly said to Brendan, "Little sisters are a real pain."

"I guess so," said Brendan. He knew his older brothers felt the same about him.

They cycled out of the yard and down the main street of the village. They asked everyone they met if they had seen Bernie, but no one had.

"I expect she's off somewhere playing with that weedy little mate of hers, Alice Ryan," said Molly. "Come on, we'd better get down to the boathouse, or else that fool Mick will come out looking for us, and give himself away."

"I wonder if they've caught that gang yet," said Brendan.

"They can't have, or it would have been on the news this morning."

They cycled down the lane to the river and turned to go along the river-bank. Suddenly Dessy jumped out of the hedge. Brendan nearly fell off his bike. They stopped.

"Dessy, what do you think you're at?" Brendan said sourly.

"Where have you been? I've been waiting for you!" Dessy said. He sounded very worried.

"What's wrong, Dessy?" asked Molly. "Has Rory run off?"

"Worse than that," said Dessy. "I went down there along the river-bank to see if I could catch a fish. Mick was really whingeing about how hungry he was. Suddenly that American woman comes up to me."

"Diane?" said Brendan.

"Yeh, that's right," said Dessy. "She asked me if I'd be seeing you and I said I might, and she told me to give you this." He held out a piece of paper. "Read it."

Brendan took the paper and read it. He looked up. His face was very anxious.

"It's about Bernie," he said. "They've kidnapped her!"

10

Kidnap

Molly took the note from Brendan. She read it out:

Your little sister is with us. She is quite safe. She will come to no harm if you come to the castle tonight and show us where the brooch is hidden. Do not, we repeat, Do Not tell your parents or the police, or you will never see your sister again.

"They're monsters!" cried Molly. "We must find them, and release Bernie."

"Maybe we should tell the guards after all," said Brendan. "They're probably bluffing."

"We daren't risk it," said Molly.

"Besides," Dessy said, "once we call the guards in, they'd get Mick as well."

"Where can they have hidden her?" Molly wondered. "Everyone round here knows her. They'd have raised the alarm."

"Mick will be raising alarms too," said Dessy, "if I

don't take him some food soon."

"Here, take this to him," said Molly, giving him the bags. "We'll start looking in all the barns and old buildings we can think of, to see if we can find where they have hidden Bernie."

They cycled back up the lane. As they reached the road, they were nearly knocked down by a car. It screeched to a stop. Mrs O'Rourke jumped out. She was in a great rage.

"Have you seen it? Have you seen it?" she yelled.

"Seen what, Mrs O'Rourke?" Molly was alarmed. It looked as if Mrs O'Rourke had gone completely mad.

"The caravan of course! The horse-rustlers have stolen it, horse and all. The people who hired it left it outside your store to get supplies, and when they came out, they saw it going off down the street."

"We haven't seen it, we were down at the river," said Brendan.

"I'm calling the guards!" shrieked Mrs O'Rourke. "This is too much! Too much altogether!" She got back into her car, crashed it into gear, and roared off up the road.

"Wow! She's really angry!" said Brendan.

Molly was frowning thoughtfully. Then she said, "That's it!"

"What's it?"

"I know who must have taken that caravan – Harry and Diane!"

"What makes you think that?" Brendan asked.

"It all fits together. Suppose they were lurking

around, near our shop, ready to waylay us, probably, when they saw Bernie come out. They snatched her up, shoved her in the caravan, and then drove off."

"How did they get the note to Dessy?"

"There's a bridge across the river, they probably saw him from there. They stopped the caravan beyond the bridge, among the trees there, and Diane came back with the note."

"It makes sense," said Brendan.

"We must follow them," said Molly.

"How will we know which way they've gone?"

"Those caravans always follow a set route. You can't make the horses go any other way."

"We'd never catch them on our bikes."

"No – but we would with another horse. Come on, let's get Rory!"

They pedalled frantically back down the lane and along the river-bank. They burst into the boathouse.

Mick was sitting on a sleeping-bag, trying to munch a sandwich with one hand, while he used the other to push away the eager mouth of Rory, who was keen to share the meal with him.

"Get him off, get him off!" said Mick.

"We're taking him!" said Molly.

"What do you mean?" asked Dessy.

Quickly, Molly and Brendan explained what had happened. "So we're going to chase them!" said Molly finally. "Come along, Rory, let's hit the trail!"

She took the end of the rope from the hook on the wall and began to lead Rory out of the boathouse.

"What about us?" said Dessy. "We won't be able to keep up."

"You stay here with Mick," said Molly. "I'm afraid Rory's back wouldn't bear more than two of us."

"*Two*!" Brendan exclaimed. "But I can't . . . "

"Come on, Brendan," said Molly. "I told you country life was more exciting than you thought."

Brendan couldn't back out now, without seeming a wimp. But the idea of riding on the back of this huge creature made his legs feel weak. Now Molly was outside the boathouse, holding the rope and patting the horse's head.

"Come on, Brendan!" she called. "We've got to hurry."

As Brendan was going out of the boathouse, he turned and saw Dessy grinning at him. "Attaboy, Brendan!" said Dessy, giving the thumbs up sign. "Ride'em cowboy!"

"Get lost!" Brendan said, and went out.

He stared at the huge beast. Rory stared back, with what Brendan thought was a look of great dislike.

"All aboard!" said Molly, leaping up on Rory's back and sitting astride him. She gazed down at Brendan, who looked as if he would rather climb Mount Everest than try to get on to the horse. "I'll tell you what," she said. "See that tree-stump along the bank? You stand up on that, and I'll bring Rory up beside it. Then you can easily climb on."

Glumly, Brendan walked to the tree-stump and stood up on it. He watched the horse lumbering towards him.

"Whoa, Rory!" said Molly, and the horse stopped obediently. "OK, Brendan, put your hands on his back, and then jump up."

Brendan reached up. He held his breath, then jumped, swinging his legs up over the horse's back. They went straight across his back and he found himself slithering down the other side of the animal, and falling in a heap on the ground.

He glared up at Molly, almost daring her to laugh. She decided to let him off lightly. "Good try, Brendan," she said. "Next time, you'll do it."

And he did. He found himself sitting up astride the horse's broad back behind Molly.

"Nice work!" she said. "Now hold on to me, and when I lean forward and we pick up speed, you lean forward too. And hold on tight and grip with your legs. It could be a bumpy ride."

They began to move along the footpath, with Rory going at a stately walk. Then they turned up the lane towards the road. The leaning fuchsia hedges brushed his knees. He could see over them into the fields beyond. He found he could balance quite well.

Horse-riding wasn't so difficult after all. Perhaps with a bit of practice he could take up a career as a jockey. He could hear the crowd roar, "Come on, Brendan! Come on!" as he streaked past the winning-post to win the Grand National.

As they joined the road, he was soon brought out of his daydream with a jolt.

"Go, Rory!" said Molly, leaning forward, and

Brendan was nearly bumped off the horse's back, as it started to trot steadily along the road. He held on, gripping with his knees, as they picked up speed.

They went over the bridge, and Brendan looked over at the river below. If he slipped in now, he'd plunge straight down into the water. He held on even tighter.

"You know the way, don't you, Rory?" Molly laughed, as they clattered up the road. They were among a belt of fir trees which rose up darkly on each side of them. The sun shone slantingly through the branches on to the dry earth below. Brendan saw a rabbit hopping along. It stopped, nose twitching.

Brendan imagined what it must be like in the jungle, where he would be travelling perhaps on an elephant, and tigers would be peering from the trees instead of rabbits.

"You're doing fine!" said Molly. "This is the life, eh?"

Brendan had to admit to himself that he was enjoying it much more than he expected. When they came out of the trees, the road began to climb slowly across scrubby land scattered with clumps of bright yellow gorse bushes. They came to the top of the rise and saw the road winding down again towards a network of fields.

There it was, in the distance: the stolen caravan.

"Giddy-up, Rory!" Molly called. The horse began to move faster and faster down the hill, and Brendan felt himself rocking from side to side.

Gradually they gained ground on the caravan. It

was barrel-shaped, and painted green and red with big yellow wooden wheels. At the back there was a window opening, with curtains drawn across it.

The caravan rattled along at a steady pace as they got nearer and nearer. Suddenly the curtains parted, and they saw Bernie's face peep out. "Hang on, Bernie!" shouted Molly. "The Ballygandon Brooch Gang's here!"

"Molly! Molly! Molly!" Bernie shrieked, waving and jumping up and down with delight. Then another face appeared behind Bernie's. It was Diane.

"Come away from there!" she snapped at Bernie, pulling her back into the caravan. They saw her turn into the inside of the caravan, and heard her shout, "Faster, Harry! Go faster!"

The caravan picked up speed, and so did Rory. It swayed from side to side, and the wheels rattled and bumped.

Suddenly it turned off the road and into a lane with trees overhanging it so that it looked like a leafy tunnel. The branches brushed the top of the caravan, and as they followed, Brendan had to duck sometimes to avoid being struck by them.

They reached the end of the lane, and before the caravan could stop, it ran into a shallow pool at the edge of a field and stuck fast in the mud.

The horse in the shafts stamped about, whinnying.

Molly reined Rory in just before he reached the edge of the pool. She and Brendan jumped down from the horse's back and ran to the back of the caravan. In the window, they could see Bernie struggling with Diane. Molly shouted, "The guards are just behind us! The game's up!"

Diane let go of Bernie, who scrambled out of the window and jumped. Brendan caught her and let her down gently to the ground. At the front of the caravan, they saw Diane emerge on to the platform where Harry was still holding the reins.

"Run for it!" yelled Diane. She and Harry climbed down from the platform and set off across the fields.

"Are you all right, Bernie?" asked Molly.

"Yes," said her sister. "They said they were just taking me for a little ride in the caravan. It was fun, but then when I said I wanted to go home, they said I couldn't. I was scared."

"It's OK, Bernie, you're safe with us now," said Brendan.

"We've seen the last of those bad people," said Molly.

"I doubt it," said Brendan. "They still haven't got the brooch, remember? My guess is they'll be back to look for it tonight in the castle – and we'll be there to meet them!"

11

Night Search

The caravan was stuck fast in the mud of the pool. It would take a tractor to lift it out. And the horse was still trapped in the shafts. It was stamping and snorting, trying to get free. Molly splashed through the water. She knew the horse. It was called Thunder and it was not nearly as good-tempered as Rory.

As Molly approached, it whinnied and reared its head. "Quiet, Thunder, quiet," she said. As she began unstrapping the shafts, the angry horse tried to twist its head back to reach her, snorting and snapping. Molly stayed well back, freed one side, then made a wide circle around the front of the horse to get to the other side.

When the final strap was freed, Thunder shook himself and stamped about in the mud, then moved forward out of the pond. He ran off across the field, crashed through the hedge, and trotted away up the road.

Molly rode Rory back the way they had come, with Bernie sitting up on the horse in front of her.

This time Brendan jogged along beside them. It was lucky all his football practice had kept him fit, but even so he wasn't too sorry when they came to a stop just at the top of the lane that led down to the river.

Molly handed Bernie down to Brendan and then got down herself.

"You run off back to Mam," said Molly. "But listen – don't say anything about the caravan trip. Not yet, anyway. We want to catch that pair red-handed at the castle tonight."

"It's a secret?" said Bernie eagerly.

"That's right," said Brendan. "A secret of the Ballygandon Brooch Gang!" He put his finger to his lips, then gave the thumbs-up sign. Giggling, Bernie did the same. Then she turned and ran off up the road.

When they led Rory back through the door of the boathouse, Mick grumbled, "Did you have to bring that brute back? I was hoping we could get the horse stink out of the place."

"We thought you'd be missing your stable-mate," grinned Brendan.

"What happened, what happened?" Dessy asked eagerly.

They told him about the caravan chase. Dessy was impressed, especially with Brendan's horse-riding. "You mean you never fell off once?" he said.

"Not at all," said Brendan. "It's easy enough,

when you've got a natural sense of how to do it."

Molly laughed and said, "He'll be joining the circus next."

"As a clown, maybe!" said Mick.

Brendan looked at him coldly. Then he said, "Now we must plan our next move. First of all we must make that phone call to the guards."

"I'm not sure they'd believe you, they get lots of hoax calls," said Molly. "I've got another idea. We'll leave a letter in Guard Delaney's house."

She explained that Emma Delaney was based at the garda station in the next village, but that she lived here in Ballygandon with her mother. Her house was down a side road off the main street, so they had a good chance of not being seen leaving the letter. There would be plenty of time for her to alert a group of gardaí to catch Harry and Diane at the castle tonight.

They wrote the note in capital letters, explaining that the brooch was hidden in the castle and that the thieves would be coming for it tonight. Then they drew a picture of the brooch so that the guards would know they weren't just fooling.

"How shall we sign it?" asked Molly.

"The Ballygandon Brooch Gang," Dessy suggested.

"That makes us sound just like the robbers," said Brendan. "Why don't we just put 'SIGNED, A FRIEND'?"

"I know!" said Molly. "How about 'FRIENDS OF THE BALLYGANDON HOARD'!"

"Great!" said Brendan. They folded the paper and wrote on the outside:

URGENT!

TO GUARD EMMA DELANEY

URGENT!

Molly and Brendan walked up to the main street with the note. At the far end, they could see Guard Delaney herself, with Mrs O'Rourke. They moved slowly along the street and loitered behind a parked van, where they could hear the conversation.

Mrs O'Rourke was angry – as usual. "It's intolerable!" she was saying. "First horse-rustlers, and then caravan-stealers! And what do you do about it? Nothing! All you're good for is giving out parking tickets. No wonder the country is the way it is."

"Calm down, Mrs O'Rourke," said Emma Delaney. "I've reported the matter, and we'll do our best to find them."

"I should hope you will!" snapped Mrs O'Rourke.

Just then, further up the street, they heard the sound of trotting hooves. They peeped out from behind the parked van. In the distance, coming towards them, was Thunder.

"I knew he'd find his way back," said Molly.

They heard Emma Delaney say, "Is this one of your horses?"

Mrs O'Rourke shouted, "It's Thunder! But he's lost his caravan!"

She moved out into the street as the horse approached, calling, "Thunder! Come here,

Thunder! Good boy!" But Thunder shied away from her and trotted off in the opposite direction. "Thunder, come here!" cried Mrs O'Rourke, running after him.

Guard Delaney looked relieved to be rid of her. Brendan and Molly were afraid she would go down the side road and home, so that they couldn't leave the note without being seen, but instead she got into her small blue car and drove off.

They came cautiously out from behind the van and hurried along the street till they came to the side road.

No one was around. They dashed down the little road to the Delaneys' door, which was directly on the street. They pushed the note through the letter box and ran up the road again.

At tea that evening, Molly's father said, "It seems the guards caught that gang they were after for the big truck theft in Dublin."

Brendan and Molly looked at each other.

"Did they get them all?" Brendan asked casually.

"There's one fella they're still looking for, I think," said Molly's father. "But they got the main ones."

Brendan and Molly wondered how they could let Mick and Dessy know. Maybe now Mick would give himself up. But they had promised to help Molly's father stack some of the new supplies in the shop. If they tried to get out of it, it could look suspicious – and they wanted to be sure they would be able to slip away later on that night.

They waited upstairs beside the window, as they had done the last time. The minutes seemed to crawl by. Tonight, dark clouds were building up in the sky, and the moon could only be glimpsed for a moment, then it would disappear behind the black curtain of cloud. The wind was getting up, too, and blowing the trees about.

The light began to fade sooner because of the clouds, and the ruined castle on the hill looked grim and desolate.

Once again, they tiptoed past the closed door of the living-room, hearing the sound of the television and the regular snores of Molly's father.

As the window rattled in the wind, they heard Molly's mother say, "It's going to be a wild night, John."

There was a grunt from her husband, and then a muttered, "What did you say?"

"Never mind, go back to sleep," said Mrs Donovan.

"I was not asleep!"

"Yes, you were."

As the argument continued, Molly and Brendan silently let themselves out the front door.

As they climbed the hill towards the castle, they felt a few drops of rain. Brendan was worried. Suppose there was a real downpour, and the earth covering the brooch was washed away? Diane and Harry might see it glinting and snatch it up. But then they still wouldn't be able to get away from the guards.

As they neared the castle, Brendan hoped the guards wouldn't see them. He was sure the police would wait till after dark before surrounding the castle, so that Harry and Diane would be inside, and wouldn't spot them and try to make a getaway.

Brendan and Molly squeezed through the gap and crept along the wall to the big fireplace. Dessy was there already, waiting for them. They crouched down beside him.

The night seemed to be full of noises. Wood creaked, and they hoped it was the trees. The wind howled around the broken walls of the castle, where once, so long ago, the wedding feast had been held – the feast that was to end with the tragic murder of Princess Ethna and the launching of a feud that would be long and bloody.

It was easy to imagine that the wind's howls were the spirits of Ethna and her family screaming for revenge.

But then, with some relief, they heard familiar human voices.

"Come on, Harry! You're moving like a snail."

"I'm carrying this silly machine, for heaven's sake!"

"Oh, give it to me!"

They were through the gap now and in the room. Brendan and Molly crouched into the back of the fireplace. They didn't dare to peer out, though they were very curious to see what on earth Harry meant by the "silly machine" he was carrying.

They saw the torch beam moving towards the

middle of the room. Now they could see the dark figures of Harry and Diane. And Diane was holding something with a handle, that looked like some sort of vacuum cleaner.

"I'll start right here," said Diane. "You take your torch and scout around to see if you can find where there's any ground that's been recently disturbed."

Harry wandered off, shining his torch on the ground, and stumbling and cursing as he tripped over loose stones.

Diane began to move the gadget slowly across the earth.

"What is it?" whispered Molly.

"I think I know," said Brendan. "It's a metal detector! The kind of thing they use to find Buried Treasure!"

12

Fear in the Ruins

"How do they work?" asked Molly.

"When they go over a place where there's metal buried, they make a kind of clicking sound," said Brendan.

Just as he spoke, they heard Harry call out, "Diane! Over here!"

"What's up?" Diane moved across the room to where Harry was bending down, shining the torch on the ground.

"See?" he said. "Just here – it looks disturbed."

"Could be," said Diane. Then she moved the detector over the spot. They could hear a metallic, crackling sound, like a radio being tuned in.

"Dig!" said Diane.

Harry produced a trowel from the pocket of his coat, knelt down, and began to dig a hole. Soon he put his hand into it and cried, "Yes, there's something here."

After more scrabbling and digging, he grabbed something from the hole and held it up. "Got it!" he said triumphantly.

"Let's have a look," said Diane, shining her torch on the object. Then she snorted and said, "Idiot! It's a rusty old tin-can. Some treasure!"

"How was I to know?" said Harry. "Your machine didn't!"

"Shut up, and keep searching," said Diane.

Huddled against the wind and the occasional flurry of rain, they went on with their search of the room. When they had finished, they moved through the ruins towards the big chamber.

"The guards should be here, by now," said Dessy. "I'll take a peep out and see if I can spot them." He crept along the wall and looked through the gap where they had come in.

"Any sign of them?" asked Brendan.

"No, I can't see anyone out there at all."

Crouching together on the ground, they wondered what had happened. Had Emma Delaney not come home and seen the note? Had her old mother thrown it away?

"Maybe they're waiting out of sight, disguised as bushes and trees," said Dessy.

"Or they want to be sure to catch Diane and Harry red-handed," said Molly.

"That's right!" said Brendan excitedly. "And we've got to make sure the guards *do* catch them red-handed, with the brooch! Otherwise they might say they were just treasure-hunting. We've got to lead

Diane and Harry to the brooch."

"Then when they've picked it up, we'll shout to the guards to come and get them," said Molly.

"Suppose there *aren't* any guards, after all?" said Dessy.

"We'll just have to take them prisoner ourselves." Brendan spoke with bravado, though they all wondered if they would be a match for Harry and Diane if it came to a struggle.

"We've got to make them go to the window end of the chamber," said Brendan.

They crept through the ruins until they were just outside the arch that led into the chamber. The window where the brooch was hidden was at the far end. Harry and Diane were searching along the side wall.

"How about conjuring up a few more ghosts?" said Molly, taking her tin whistle out of her anorak pocket.

"Good idea," said Brendan. "You do the wailing with that, and Dessy and I can do some ghostly screams and laughs."

"Don't overdo it," Molly warned. She knew Brendan well enough now to realise that his enthusiasm sometimes went a bit wild. She put the tin whistle to her lips. Out came the low, moaning wail.

They saw Harry and Diane stop and look around.

"Did you hear that?" asked Harry. Molly made the sound again.

"It's the wind," said Diane, sounding unsure of herself.

Brendan gave a high, eerie scream. Dessy made a mad chuckle.

Molly put her fingers to her lips, and they all stayed quiet.

"That was no wind," said Harry with a shudder. "I tell you the place is haunted!"

"Nonsense!" Diane's voice was quavering. Molly made the wailing sound again, and Brendan and Dessy made their noises.

"It came from over there," said Harry, pointing at the arch. "I'm getting out of here." He looked around wildly. Then he realised that the archway was the only entrance to the big chamber. He backed away down the room, tripping over stones and rocks. Diane moved with him. They were almost at the far end now, where the empty, arched window towered above them.

The three made their ghostly sounds once more. Harry and Diane were now backed against the wall, just under the window. Harry reached up to the window-ledge.

"Maybe we can climb out this way," he said, trying to jump, and coming down to earth again. "Diane, give me a leg up."

"No – I'll go first," said Diane. She reached up to the window-ledge, her feet pushing at the ground below, just in the area where the brooch was buried.

"Wait!" said Harry. "Look at that, beside your foot. I'm sure I saw something bright." Brendan, Molly and Dessy looked at each other and smiled.

Diane and Harry were kneeling down under the

big window, beside the wall. Harry dug with his trowel, and Diane pushed earth aside with her bare hands. Then they heard Diane shriek.

"Something cut me!" she said, looking at her hand.

"I knew that brooch had a curse on it," Dessy whispered. "Princess Ethna strikes again!"

Harry reached into the hole and slowly held up the brooch. Then he shouted, "We got it! We got it!"

"Yes, indeed!" said Diane. "That's it!" She forgot her cut hand as she gazed at the brooch greedily. Then she took it from Harry, carefully, and stared at it.

"Those kids must have hidden it here," said Harry. "They never thought we'd find it. Now let's get out of here."

"Time to get the guards," said Molly.

"I'll run out and tell them," said Brendan. "If we shout, those two may run for it. Keep them in here with a few more ghost noises."

Just then they saw Diane move towards the archway.

"Not that way!" said Harry.

"Oh, bother the ghosts! I'm getting out." She was coming in their direction. Molly made another wailing sound with her tin whistle, and Dessy gave a deep groan.

Harry said in a quaking voice, "I can't face it, Diane. I'm going out the window."

"OK." Diane sounded quite relieved not to have to come through the arch. She moved back to the window and started trying to help Harry up. But he kept tumbling back, nearly knocking her down.

Meanwhile, Brendan crept back through the ruins to the gap where they had come in. He squeezed through it and looked around. The trees sighed and rustled in the wind, and the clouds whirled and eddied across the night sky. But Brendan could see no sign of any human being.

He moved around the castle on the outside. He could see no one. What could have gone wrong? He would have to go down to the village and see if he could find Emma Delaney, or else he'd have to ring the guards himself. He went back into the ruins to tell Molly and Dessy.

As he reached them, he could see that Harry and Diane, at the far end of the chamber, were still trying without success to clamber up through the window. He explained that there was no sign of the guards, and that he'd have to go down to the village.

He turned to make his way back. Then he stopped still, and felt his body go suddenly cold. In the doorway which led back into the room where he'd come in stood a dark, hooded figure in a long cloak.

Molly and Dessy had seen it too. They all stared. The figure stood still, in the doorway, for a long time. Brendan, Molly and Dessy shrank back against the wall, in the shadows.

Dessy whispered, "It's her! Princess Ethna!"

All three of them stayed quite still, staring at the

strange, ghostly apparition. As they gazed, it began to glide slowly forward across the ground. It was looking straight ahead at the archway that led into the chamber. From the far end of the chamber, they could hear Diane and Harry, still grunting and cursing as they tried to get up to the window.

The figure got to the archway and stopped at the entrance to the chamber. They could hear the scrabbling sounds and the voices of Harry and Diane. Suddenly the noises ceased. There was a terrified scream from Diane, and a loud, groaning wail from Harry.

"It's the Ghost!" he cried. Then there was silence. They could hear Harry sobbing and whimpering. Diane was speechless.

The figure advanced slowly into the chamber. The wind rose and howled around the ruined castle walls. In the midst of it they seemed to hear a mournful sighing, like someone in the very depths of grief.

They crept along the wall and peered round the corner of the archway. The figure was advancing towards the cowering pair under the window. Diane had flattened herself back against the wall. Harry was on his knees, sobbing.

The figure stopped. A voice came from under the hood, sharp and menacing, "I'll be revenged on you!"

"No! No! No!" Harry wailed. "It was all her idea."

"Traitor!" snarled Diane.

"Revenged!" said the figure.

Diane held out the brooch. "Take it! Take it!" she screeched.

"Bring it to me."

Haltingly, Diane moved across the uneven floor, the brooch held out in front of her. As she reached the figure, a hand reached out from under the cloak and snatched the brooch. There was a muffled cry.

"You jabbed me!" snapped the voice beneath the hood.

"It's the brooch, it's got a curse on it!" moaned Harry.

Then they heard Diane say sharply, "Jabbed you? How could I jab a ghost?"

She grabbed the hood and pulled it away. Then she stepped back with a gasp of surprise. "You!" she said.

"Yes, me!"

Brendan, Molly and Dessy stared with equal astonishment. They recognised the head of the cloaked figure. It was Mrs O'Rourke.

13

Revenge

"It's you!" Diane gasped again.

"It is indeed," said Mrs O'Rourke menacingly.

"Thank God," Harry whimpered, creakily getting up from his knees, "I thought it was the ghost of that Princess."

"By the time I've finished with you, you're going to wish it was the ghost instead of me."

"They know each other," whispered Brendan to Molly.

"And she knew about the brooch," said Molly. "They must be all in it together, the theft and everything."

"But why didn't Harry and Diane link up with her before now?" Dessy wondered. They soon heard the answer.

"You double-crossing bastards!" yelled Mrs O'Rourke. "I should have known when I hired you, you couldn't be trusted."

"We were going to bring the brooch to you right away, like you said," whined Diane. "But then those kids stole it, and we had to track it down."

"And if they hadn't taken it, I'd never have heard from you again!" said Mrs O'Rourke sourly. "You planned to leave Dublin at once, didn't you, and catch the next plane out of the country? With the brooch *and* the money I paid you to steal it."

"Listen to that!" said Brendan. "They've confessed the whole plot! You must keep them here somehow, while I go and get the guards."

But just then Mrs O'Rourke snapped, "Get over there, by the archway."

"You've got the brooch, what more do you want?" said Diane.

"I want my money back," said Mrs O'Rourke.

"We're not giving it back," said Diane, "we risked our necks, stealing that brooch for you."

"And I'll *break* your necks, if you don't give it to me," Mrs O'Rourke sounded furious now, "I said I'd be revenged on you, and I will!"

"You can't touch us, without giving yourself away," said Diane.

"Oh no?" shouted Mrs O'Rourke. "Well, see how you like *this*!"

From under her cloak she produced a whip and cracked it in the air.

Diane and Harry froze. There was a silence. Then Mrs O'Rourke said sharply, "Get over there, against the wall!"

They obeyed her at once, rushing and stumbling

over the rough ground, with Mrs O'Rourke stalking behind them, the whip raised. Soon, Diane and Harry were against the wall, just the other side of the archway from where Brendan, Molly and Dessy stood. Mrs O'Rourke was facing the archway.

If Brendan tried to sneak away now to get the guards, she would certainly see him. The only thing they could do was to stay where they were and keep quiet.

"The money!" snapped Mrs O'Rourke. She gave a crack of the whip. Harry began to whimper.

"Here's all I've got left," Harry whimpered. They heard the rustle of some notes, and a clatter of coins on the stones of the floor.

"And you!" said Mrs O'Rourke to Diane, with another crack of the whip.

"We spent most of it, it's gone," said Diane. "Here's all I've got."

"Give me that bag!" The whip cracked again. "I said, give it to me!"

"OK, OK . . . "

"Now let's have a look," said Mrs O'Rourke. Then she gave a sneering laugh. "Gone, is it? What's this then? You're still trying to double-cross me! Well, this is the last time you'll think of doing that. They used to horse whip villains in the old days. I dare say they did a lot of it in this very castle. Time the punishment was revived, don't you think?"

She gave another cackle of laughter, and the whip cracked again. Harry and Diane both screamed, and then Diane cried, "Run for it!"

Brendan, Molly and Dessy flattened themselves back against the wall, as Harry and Diane ran through the archway, followed by Mrs O'Rourke, lashing out with the whip. They ran into the next room and over to the far side where the gap was in the outer wall.

As she rushed after them, Mrs O'Rourke tripped on her cloak and fell sprawled on the ground. She cursed and swore as she started to get up.

"Hurry, hurry, for God's sake!" Diane cried, pushing a grunting Harry through the gap. Mrs O'Rourke struggled up and rushed towards her. Diane squeezed through the gap as the whip cracked behind her. Mrs O'Rourke decided not to follow. She stood with the whip in her hand, gazing after them.

Then she turned.

"She's coming back this way," said Molly. They crouched back against the wall in the shadow and saw the cloaked figure stop just at the doorway of the room. She held the whip in one hand, and then held the other hand out in front of her. In her palm lay Princess Ethna's brooch.

She gazed at it for a long time. Then they heard her sigh and say triumphantly to herself, "Mine! Mine at last!"

She raised her head and looked up at the jagged walls of the castle, rising up against the night sky. The wind was still blowing in fierce gusts, but the rain had stopped and the moon shone out now and then between the clouds that raced across the sky.

"I have it, Princess! Your brooch is mine now!"

Mrs O'Rourke called. "And when the fuss dies down, I'll make a fortune from it. But for now, I'll leave it in your castle, for safe keeping!"

They saw her look around, and heard her say softly, "But where? Where . . . "

She wandered on into the room beyond, still holding the brooch before her.

"We must follow her," said Molly.

"What about the guards?" Dessy asked.

"By the time we get them, she'll have hidden the brooch," said Brendan. "We must see where she hides it, and then we can lead the guards to it, and tell them what we saw. If the three of us swear to it, they'll have to believe us."

They crept across the floor and peered around the corner of the doorway to the next room. Mrs O'Rourke was standing in the middle of the room, still wondering where to hide the brooch.

"Maybe we could run at her and over power her," Dessy suggested.

"It's a bit dodgy," said Brendan. "She's got the whip, remember."

They saw Mrs O'Rourke looking towards the far corner of the room. There was the remains of a tower in this corner, with a narrow doorway leading into it. The beginnings of a stone staircase could be seen, spiralling upwards inside. The tower had been much taller, but now it was only about thirty metres high, and the stones at the top were broken and jagged. There was a gap, where they could see the staircase ending in empty air.

Mrs O'Rourke went purposefully across to the entrance to the tower. She paused, then went in and began to climb the stairs.

"We can't follow her up there," said Molly, "she'd see us."

"But we know she's hidden it somewhere in the tower," said Brendan. "It shouldn't be hard for the guards to find."

They waited for a while, expecting to see Mrs O'Rourke come out of the tower door again. But instead, they heard a scream from inside the tower. Then there was a cry of, "No! No! Stay there! Don't come near me! Please! Please!"

There was a choking cry, and then Mrs O'Rourke appeared at the top of the tower stairway, just where it ended, opening on to nothing.

She clutched the broken wall and stood there, staring back down the stairway. She was terrified. She seemed to be shouting at someone coming up the stairs after her. But they had seen no one follow her in.

Mrs O'Rourke certainly seemed to see someone. And as they watched, they thought they saw a strange light inside the tower. It glowed in the entrance way and through the cracks in the side of the tower, and seemed even to throw a beam of light on Mrs O'Rourke's face, as she gazed in terror down the stairs behind her.

"Don't hurt me!" screamed Mrs O'Rourke. "I'll give you back your brooch! Take it! Please, Princess, please!" She was kneeling down now, right at the edge of the last stair. If she leaned backwards, she would plunge down on to the rocky ground below.

They watched, mouths open, their hair prickling on their heads. The light glowed more intensely. Could it be a trick of the moonlight? It looked too bright for that.

Mrs O'Rourke was sure it was no trick. She was sighing and sobbing and pleading.

"I only wanted it as my right! *I* should have found the Ballygandon Hoard! *I* should have got the money for it! But I don't want now. Spare me, and take the brooch! Take it!"

With a cry, she flung the brooch back down the stairs. She knelt there at the top, sobbing. They thought they heard a long, deep sigh come from the direction of the tower. The light inside dimmed and disappeared.

Mrs O'Rourke was still rooted to the spot, sobbing and clinging to the stone wall, when they heard the scrabbling of feet among the ruins. Torches began to flash around the crumbling walls.

They heard voices.

"Where are they then?" said a gruff man's voice.

Then a woman's voice said, "The note just said that the brooch was hidden in the castle, and that the robbers would come for it tonight."

Molly recognised Emma Delaney's voice. "It's here, it's here!" Molly called.

The torch beams shone into the room. Guard Delaney came in with two other guards. They shone the torches on the three figures in the centre of the room.

"It's you, Molly!" said Emma.

"Yes," said Molly. "And there's the thief!" She pointed at the tower. The torched beamed upwards.

In their spotlight was the kneeling, cloaked figure of Mrs O'Rourke, shielding her eyes from the glare.

14

The Final Chase

"Stay there, you'll be all right," said one of the guards, seeing Mrs O'Rourke begin to sway a little on the ledge. "We're coming up to bring you down."

He and Emma Delaney moved across the entrance to the tower. They shone their torches inside.

Mrs O'Rourke screamed down the stairway, "Keep her away! I gave her back the brooch I stole! Keep her away from me!"

"Keep *who* away?" asked Emma. "There's no one here."

"The Ghost! The Princess! I saw her!" Mrs O'Rourke sobbed.

"There's no ghost," said the other guard. "Just keep calm. We'll bring you down."

The two guards entered the tower. They heard Emma exclaim, "Here it is! The stolen brooch. Lying on the stairway."

They saw Emma at the top of the stairs, beside Mrs O'Rourke. Gently, she persuaded her to get up, then she took her hand and led her down the stairs.

As they came out of the tower doorway, Emma Delaney said, "You see – there was nothing there."

"I saw her! I saw her!" Mrs O'Rourke cried.

"I'll look after her," said the third guard. "You get after the other two." He took Mrs O'Rourke's arm and guided her across the broken floor, saying "I'll wait in the car with her, and then we can take them all to the station to be charged."

They moved away, out of the castle and down the hill. Emma and the other guard took another path down, and Brendan, Molly and Dessy went with them.

Emma explained that she hadn't gone home and found the note until about an hour ago. Then she had called for reinforcements and come straight up to the castle. She told Molly that they would probably get the reward which had been offered for recovering the brooch.

"Great! We can afford to keep Rory," said Molly.

"Rory?" said Emma. "Isn't that the horse Mrs O'Rourke said had been stolen?"

"Well . . . " said Molly.

"Do you know where he is?"

"Not exactly . . . " said Brendan.

They had reached the bottom of the hill now. "Anyway," said Emma, "we'll worry about the horse later. It's the *human* suspects we're after now. Which way do you reckon they'd have gone, Joe?"

The other guard said, "They'd keep off the roads, I'd say. Maybe they'd try to get away along the river-bank."

Molly, Brendan and Dessy looked at each other with some dismay. If the guards went along the river-bank, they might look in the boathouse and discover not just Rory, but Mick as well. Perhaps they could go ahead and warn them.

When they got to the river-bank, Brendan said, "We'll go ahead a bit, shall we, and see if we can see anything." The three of them began to hurry off along the path.

"Wait!" said the guard called Joe. "What's that noise up ahead there?"

They all stopped and listened.

Ahead, just where the river curved to the spot where the boathouse was, they heard the sound of voices shouting. Then there was a crashing sound, and the whinnying of a horse.

"Let's go!" said Joe. They all started running along the path, until they rounded the corner. They could hear the voices clearly now. They were coming from the boathouse.

"No, you cannot stay here!" shouted Mick.

Then they heard Diane shouting back, "We'll stay where we like!"

"It's a free country," said Harry.

"And keep your voice down," said Diane.

"*You* keep your voice down!" yelled Mick.

There was a whinny from Rory.

"And shut that horse up, too!" said Harry.

The two guards rushed to the boathouse and flung open the door. They all looked in. Diane, Harry and Mick were standing in the middle of the room, gesturing and shouting, Rory was by one of the walls, pawing the ground and snorting. When they saw the guards at the door, with Brendan, Molly and Dessy behind them, the three stopped still, staring at the group in the doorway.

Then Mick cursed and said, "I'm getting out of here!" He looked around wildly, then took hold of the horse's mane and tried to jump on his back. Rory reared up on his hind legs, and Mick slid off and was left sitting in the mud.

"I had nothing to do with it, I stole no treasure," Mick said pleadingly.

"You'd nothing to do with the treasure, maybe," said Joe. "But I think you can help us with another inquiry."

Dessy realised that Mick might have changed his mind about giving himself up when the rest of the gang had been caught. But he knew things would be better for Mick if he did come clean – especially now that there was no chance of escape.

Dessy said, "That's what you were going to do, Mick, wasn't it?"

"What?" Mick growled.

"You know," said Dessy. "Help with their inquiries. You were going to tell them all about it." He went across and glared at his brother. "You were, weren't you, Mick?" Then he whispered, "It's your best chance. You can't get away."

Mick looked at him uncertainly, then said, "That's right, I want to make a statement."

"We'll bring you down to the station, with these two, then," said Joe.

"We're not going!" said Harry.

"It'll be better if you do," said Emma. "You can't escape."

"Oh no? Just watch me!" Harry said.

He went across towards the little quay, where the boat was moored.

"Come on, Diane!" he said.

"You can't sail in that," she said.

"Come on!" said Harry. "It's our only chance!" He jumped into the boat, his feet making a splash in the water that filled the bottom of it. He began to sway about, trying to keep his balance. Then there was a splintering sound, as his weight broke the rotten planks and his feet went through the bottom of the boat. He sank in up to his waist, and stood there, flapping his arms about.

"You fool!" said Diane.

"Help me out! Help me out!" cried Harry. He was still flapping his arms and swaying. Then he lost his balance altogether and fell down on his back in the waterlogged boat. He lay there, soaking wet, in the bottom of the boat, looking like a big baby in a sunken pram.

"Get him out of there," said Joe, who couldn't help smiling.

"Me?" said Diane.

"Unless you want to leave him to drown," said Joe.

Reluctantly, Diane stepped into the shallow water and helped Harry get to his feet. They both splashed their way out of the river and stood dripping on the quay.

"You'd better come with us," Emma said to Molly. "We'll need a statement from you, too."

"What about Rory?" said Brendan.

"I'll take him back up to the field," said Molly. "He'll be safe there now." Before Emma could say anything, Molly leaped on to Rory's back and trotted away down the path.

Emma led the way out of the boathouse, and the others followed. Dessy was trying to reassure Mick, who was cursing and grumbling. Diane was whimpering to Harry, who walked along grimly, his wet clothes making a sloshing sound as he went. Joe came behind them, keeping a sharp eye on the strange little procession. Brendan followed at the end, thinking of his future career as a detective, when he'd be constantly rounding up criminals, just like this.

"Another case cracked, O'Hara," his chief would say, as Brendan led them into the station. "I don't know how you do it!"

"Nothing to it, sir," Brendan would reply, with a smile.

When they had made their statements, the guards drove them back to Ballygandon, keeping Mrs O'Rourke, Diane, Harry and Mick in the cells, ready to be taken up to Dublin the next morning.

The guards had telephoned Molly's mother and

father to tell where Brendan and Molly were. Her father tried to tell them off for sneaking out in the middle of the night, but soon he was joining her mother in praising them for their bravery and their skill in helping to solve the crime.

They said Dessy could stay with them and sleep in the other bunk bed in Brendan's room.

They phoned Brendan's parents to tell them all about it. Then Molly's mother held out the phone to Brendan and said, "Your father would like a word with you, Brendan."

Brendan took the phone nervously. He expected another telling-off from his father. But he was pleasantly surprised.

"Congratulations, Brendan!" his father said. "You're a brave lad. And maybe your friend Dessy is not so bad, after all."

"Thanks, Dad," said Brendan. "Listen, maybe if I told you everything that happened, you could use it in the story you're writing for the paper."

"Wonderful!" said his father. "I've got my notebook right here. Go ahead and give me the details. I'll mention your name, of course, and Molly's and Dessy's. This will be a real scoop! I'm very proud of you, Brendan."

Next day they were in the paper, all three of them, in a front-page story written by Brendan's father. A photographer rang to say he wanted to get a picture of them for the evening papers. They would be photographed in front of the ruined castle.

"Maybe you could get Princess Ethna's ghost in

the photo, too!" said Molly's father, laughing.

Brendan, Molly and Dessy smiled nervously. It wasn't the kind of joke that appealed to them, not after last night's strange events.

Brendan thought how he had hated the idea of a holiday in the country – but this had been the most exciting time of his life. The Ballygandon Brooch Gang was famous. He and Molly and Dessy had had the adventure of a lifetime. They had made a great team – and who could know what other adventures they might have together in the future?

Also by Poolbeg

Shiver!

Discover the identity of the disembodied voice singing haunting tunes in the attic of a long abandoned house . . .

Read about Lady Margaret de Deauville who was murdered in 1814 and discover the curse of her magic ring . . .

Who is the ghoulish knight who clambers out of his tomb unleashing disease and darkness upon the world?

Witness a family driven quietly insane by an evil presence in their new house . . .

What became of the hideous voodoo doll which disappeared after Niamh flung it from her bedroom window?

An atmospheric and suspense-filled collection of ghostly tales by fifteen of Ireland's most popular writers: Rose Doyle, Michael Scott, Jane Mitchell, Michael Mullen, Morgan Llywelyn, Gretta Mulrooney, Michael Carroll, Carolyn Swift, Mary Regan, Gordon Snell, Mary Beckett, Eileen Dunlop, Maeve Friel, Gaby Ross and Cormac MacRaois.

Each tale draws you into a web at times menacing, at times refreshingly funny.

Also by Poolbeg

Into the 21st Century

In February of this year, Ray D'Arcy of RTE's Den TV invited younger viewers to imagine what life would be like in the next century. This MS READaTHON/Den TV anthology, *Into The Twenty-First Century*, features a wonderful range of stories and styles for all ages and tastes. These young writers tackle diverse themes; some foreseeing a bleak future for the human race if threats to the environment are not faced now, others revelling in the technology of a world which features flying bikes and robot schoolteachers.

In these stories there is the sense of excitement all writers feel when they plunge into the imaginary world of their own creation. Included in this wide range is adventure, romance, suspense, drama and comedy.

With an introduction by Gordon Snell